For my very own 'Thistle Pixie - SGP',
who's always there for me,
and for the greatest storyteller in the world,
my Dad.

Contents

Chapter 1

Dream Crashers

"One horn-toed goblin, two horn-toed goblins, three horn-toed goblins," Thumble Tumble sang to herself, wriggling her toes. But her sleep song wasn't working. The evening air was so muggy it was keeping her awake. Even though it was nearly ten o'clock at night, the sun's rays beamed through the window of her tiny bedroom in the whitewashed cottage where she lived with her two aunts.

Thumble Tumble pulled the sheet right up over her head and snuggled down in bed. She got up to a hundred horn-toed goblins before she finally drifted off into a sleep that was not at all restful, because in her dream she could hear goblins chanting "Heave ho, heave ho" – which was rather strange, as the goblins in her dream were all fast asleep.

Pulling back the sheet and with her head still on the pillow, Thumble Tumble opened her left eye and scanned the room. There was no one there. Before long, she was back in the world of snoozing goblins.

"Heave ho, heave ho," the chanting persisted.

The noise was even ruining the tranquillity of the goblins in her dream, who were now waking up with grumpy frowns on their faces. Thumble Tumble sat up in bed, with an equally grumpy expression on her own face.

She looked around the room, scrutinising every nook and cranny. This time, she noticed that the window was slightly ajar and that the noise was coming from outside. "How rude," she thought.

Still half asleep, she crawled out of bed intending to close the window tight shut. First, she peered out to see who was responsible for the persistent chanting.

The culprits were four Thistle Pixies, who were marching up the hill, dragging a huge grey net behind them.

"What on earth are those guys up to?" Thumble Tumble thought curiously. She opened the window fully and leaned out to get a better look.

"Heave ho, heave ho," the Thistle Pixies repeated in unison, keeping time with their marching pace. They had made their way across the sea from the Holy Isle in a tiny rowing boat that was now docked on the beach at the bottom of Thumble Tumble's road.

Thumble Tumble watched in silence so as not to spook them. She could remember her last encounter with Thistle Pixies, and the head-bursting screech they could utter if upset.

Instead of the usual grass stain covering their bodies, she noticed that this group had smothered themselves in dirt to help them blend into the night. Even though the sun had now almost set and it was getting dark outside, the camouflage did nothing to hide them, particularly as they passed her whitewashed cottage.

Thumble Tumble stepped back from the window and slipped on a dress and a pair of shoes. She turned the star-shaped handle on her bedroom door very slowly, to avoid it creaking, then tiptoed as quietly as she could down the stairs, so as not to wake her aunts, Bessie and Isla. She had lived with them most of her life, as her parents had died when she was just a baby.

Just as she reached the bottom step, there was a loud "meow".

"Shh, Flopsy," she whispered to her little pink cat. "I'm sorry... I didn't see your tail down there."

Flopsy glared up at Thumble Tumble for a split second, then put his cheek against her leg and rubbed his face on it. He could never stay angry with Thumble Tumble for any length of time... not even when she was sneaking out in the middle of the night and had just stood on his tail.

Before leaving the cottage, Thumble Tumble got her cloak from the cupboard under the stairs. "I'll not need my broom," she thought as she pulled the red cloak off its hook and slipped it over her head.

"You go back upstairs, Flopsy," she murmured. Exiting through the magic porthole in the front door of the cottage, she started following the Thistle Pixies up the hill.

"Eyes front, hair tall and *heave*," called out Scoutt, the leader of the group. A particularly feisty Thistle Pixie, Scoutt was captain of their Eagalach team (Eagalach being the Thistle Pixies' national sport). His purple hair had thin streaks of blue through it that glowed every time he shouted out his orders. He was now ranting so much that his hair was flashing on and off like a siren.

"Are we nearly there?" groaned Lazy Bones (known as LB for short). LB had been sneakily holding on to the net whilst the other pixies pulled him up the hill. He was utterly exhausted, and very annoyed that he couldn't doze off for twenty winks because of the blue lights flashing out from the top of Scoutt's head.

"No, not yet," snapped Snoddy.

Snoddy also played for the Thistle Pixie Eagalach team, which is how he had ended up in his current predicament.

"If you would help *pull* the net, instead of just hanging off the back of it we might get there a bit faster," he added, having just noticed what LB was up to.

"I'm trying!" exclaimed LB. "Honestly… I just can't keep up."

"It would help if you tried walking instead of lying on your belly," Snoddy shot back.

He was so busy arguing with LB that he let go of the net as well.

Rocky, the fourth member of the group, was the keeper for the Eagalach team. Stockier than his three friends, he had bulging biceps and was by far the strongest of the Thistle Pixies. He did not take kindly to being the only pixie left to pull the unwieldy net up the hill.

"A little help, guys!" he yelled.

"I'm sorry," said Snoddy, guiltily seizing hold of the net. LB did not follow suit. Instead he lounged back on the net, as though he was settling into a hammock for a snooze.

As their leader, Scoutt was being extra vigilant on this evening's mission to Blakk Cemetery. He had been inside the haunted graveyard before and, unlike his companions, knew just how dangerous it was to venture there at night.

On the brow of the hill, he held up his right hand to indicate to the others to stop, but the flashing lights from his hair were so bright they couldn't see properly and as a result Rocky cannoned straight into his back.

"I gave the sign to stop," Scoutt yelped, winded by the impact.

"Apologies, Scoutt. Couldn't see you there," said Rocky, trying not to smirk. "Any chance you could switch off your hair lights?"

"We'll all need to cover our hair from here on," Scoutt snapped back, handing Rocky something that resembled a sack. "The Creepers will see *your* fancy bouffant a mile away."

Rocky opened the sack to reveal a pointy black hat. "A *gnome's* hat!" he exclaimed in disgust. "I'm not wearing this thing! It'll ruin my hairstyle."

"Not laughing now!" Snoddy said sneakily to Rocky.

"And neither are you," said Scoutt, handing Snoddy his hat.

Snoddy's smirk turned to a frown as he pulled it on.

"Where's LB?" asked Scoutt.

"I think he must have fallen off the net a bit further down the hill," Snoddy volunteered.

"Oh well, I suppose we'll pick him up on the way back," said Scoutt in a resigned tone. With that, he went down on his hands and knees and started crawling along the ground.

"What's he up to?" Rocky whispered.

"I'm not sure," replied Snoddy under his breath, "but I think we'd better follow him."

The three pixies had only travelled a few feet along the path into Blakk Cemetery when they heard a grunting sound behind them.

They froze on the spot.

The grunting got louder and louder as the unknown creature approached. And so they were all very relieved when the next thing they heard was LB's voice.

"Wait up!" he shouted, grunting and panting, out of breath from walking a full twenty yards along the path unaided.

"For goodness sake, be quiet. Do you want the Creepers to hear us?" scolded Scoutt.

Thumble Tumble stood watching the Thistle Pixies from the shadow of the cemetery wall. She listened closely as Scoutt ranted on at LB in as quiet a voice as he could muster.

"If you wake up the Creepers you'll know all about it," he warned.

He was so uptight that the blue streaks in his hair were now glowing so brightly, they were penetrating the gnome's hat he was wearing, making him look as if he had a black, cone-shaped head covered in luminous blue veins.

LB, Snoddy and Rocky stood stock still, staring in Scoutt's direction. But it wasn't his strange appearance that had caused their jaws to drop. It was the creature rising out of the ground behind him.

Chapter 2

Troll Trap

Blade was fluttering near the Lily Pond waiting for Boris to show up. They had arranged to race across the pond at midnight. It was now half past and there was no sign of Boris.

"Where on earth can he be?" Blade thought to himself. "Typical! I get up in the middle of the night, and Boris has forgotten."

Blade had already completed three warm-up laps around the pond and was now stretching each of his eight tiny wings, limbering up for the race.

"Come to think about it – where is everybody else?" he asked himself out loud.

None of the usual racing crowd had turned up.

The other Flower Nymphs didn't agree with Blade's crazy racing habits, but he had his own groupies who usually showed up to cheer him on. Tonight, even Aggie the plant-eater was missing, and she had never been known to miss a race. She had even sneaked away early from her little brother's hatching to see Blade race against

Conan, the Large Blue Butterfly, the day they flew to the top of Goatfell mountain.

The pimples on Blade's back began to throb. That was a warning sign he never ignored. Feeling nervous and wary, he fluttered down to the ground and took cover under some water reeds sprouting out of a muddy patch of grass.

There was a strange aroma coming off the mud. Blade jumped back as he realised it wasn't mud beside him, it was troll droppings!

His entire body went rigid, then sharp thorns pierced through his skin, covering him head to toe like a pincushion.

As he stood in silence under the reeds, desperately trying not to inhale the fumes from the Troll poo, he felt the ground start to tremble under his feet.

"Where do you think he is?" boomed Ogg.

Ogg was a Tree Troll. He and his twin brother Ugg were circling the pond in search of someone. Tree Trolls are notoriously stupid and Ugg and Ogg were no exception.

Ogg stood three metres tall. He was extremely thin with arms and legs that resembled branches, and a torso that looked like a tree trunk. In fact, if it wasn't for his huge head, you could easily have mistaken him for a tree. His head looked almost alien, with black, oval-shaped eyes and a round mouth.

Ugg looked identical to Ogg except that he had a stump instead of a foot at the end of his left leg.

"Maybe the dragonfly was lying," suggested Ugg. "Perhaps he's not meant to be racing the Flower Nymph at all."

"Well we can't exactly check with him, can we?"

15

burped Ogg.

"He's got to be here somewhere. Mogdred wouldn't have sent us here if he wasn't," said Ugg. "Let's split up. I'll go this way." He pointed to the pond with his right hand. "And you go that way," he continued, pointing towards the pond again, but this time with his left hand.

Ugg waddled off towards the pond and Ogg fell in behind him.

After a few steps, Ugg rounded on his brother.

"Why are you following me?" he shouted.

"But you *told* me to go this way," complained Ogg.

"Look, you go *that* way and I'll go *this* way," Ugg muttered tersely.

"OK," nodded Ogg.

The result was not what either Troll expected, for they immediately barged straight into one another, the impact of their enormous heads knocking them both off their feet.

Blade couldn't believe what he was seeing. He had heard how stupid Tree Trolls were, but this was the first time he'd actually witnessed them in action. He clenched his hands over his mouth to prevent himself from laughing as they writhed around on the ground, nursing their bruised heads.

As the Trolls struggled to pick themselves up. Blade began to tiptoe backwards away from the pond.

"Hello, my pretty," said a voice close to his left ear.

The foul stench of Mogdred's breath was far worse than Troll dung. It was so vile that Blade almost passed out. But the ghastly stench didn't invade his nostrils for long, for the evil Night Witch had lowered a large jar over his body, trapping him inside a glass prison.

Chapter 3

Blakk Cemetery

"OK," said Scoutt, "the head joke's no longer funny, guys."

Rocky, Snoddy and LB continued staring, with a look of terror in their eyes.

Without warning, Scoutt dashed towards them, pushed them to the ground and lay over them, using his body like a protective blanket.

"Close your eyes," he screamed, and all four Thistle Pixies shut their eyes.

Scoutt could feel a tingling sensation across his back for a few seconds, then it stopped. He tentatively turned his head.

"It's gone," he gasped, clambering off his friends' crumpled bodies.

"What was that... thing?" panted Snoddy, unwrapping LB's clinging arms from around his waist and picking himself up off the ground.

"That was a Creeper," replied Scoutt. "Quick, we need to get out of here. They can't leave the cemetery walls,"

he explained, hauling Rocky on to his feet.

The four pixies took off and soon darted out of the gates and fell onto the grass.

"A Creeper?" LB asked when he had got his breath back. "What in the world is a Creeper?"

"Creepers are not from this world," Scoutt said in a sombre tone. "They're from the Afterworld. They are the Living Dead."

"My goodness – do they eat brains?" yelped LB.

"No… that's just an old wives' tale," said Scoutt. "The Creepers want to come back to life and the only way they have to do that is to take someone's soul."

"That's even worse!" cried LB.

"Shh," whispered Scoutt, placing his index finger against lips. "We don't want to wake any more of them."

"But how did they get into Blakk Cemetery in the first place?" murmured Rocky.

"It all happened a long time ago…" Scoutt began. And this is the story he told.

The mansion house behind the cemetery used to be home to Lord and Lady Blakk. The handsome young couple were blissfully happy. They lived without a care in the world, until one day Lady Blakk was struck down with a mysterious illness.

Lord Blakk sought advice from every magical creature on Arran, but nothing worked and it wasn't long before his beautiful young wife died. He was heartbroken and took to spending each night by her graveside, crying.

One evening, a man visited the cemetery and told Lord Blakk there was a way to bring his wife back from the dead, but that it would cost him his own soul when he died. Lord Blakk was so desperate to see his lovely Paulianna again that he agreed to the man's terms.

Several nights passed and nothing happened. Then, on the thirteenth night after the man's visit, Lord Blakk was roused at midnight by strange noises coming from the cemetery. As he ran through the gates, he thought he could see the figure of a woman moving towards him.

"Paulianna, is that you?" he called out as he advanced deeper into the cemetery.

"Good evening, Lord Blakk," a familiar voice echoed behind him.

He turned. There stood the man with whom he'd made the terrible pact.

"Where's Paulianna?" he asked.

"She's here," the man replied, gesturing towards the ground.

Lord Blakk realised he must be standing right on top of Paulianna's grave.

"We made a pact," he shouted.

"And I have honoured it," jeered the man.

As he spoke, a woman's body rose up from the grave.

"Paulianna!" Lord Blakk cried, reaching out to embrace his wife. But Paulianna's eyes remained closed and her body was ice cold.

"What have you done to her?" howled Lord Blakk.

"I have brought her back from the dead," the stranger cackled. "I didn't say she would be alive… just back from the dead!"

As he spoke the man cranked his neck to the side and revealed himself as the Dark Wizard, Bizaldo, Lord of the Dead.

"You tricked me," said Lord Blakk, enraged. Rounding on the Dark Wizard, he drew a small dagger from his belt and held it at Bizaldo's throat.

Just then Paulianna called out his name…

"Alasdair!"

Her arms were outstretched towards him. As he leaned in to hold her, she opened her eyes – and Lord Blakk's soul was taken.

Scoutt finished his story with a small curtsy.

"So, if they take your soul, they come to life," Snoddy said, horrified.

"Yes," replied Scoutt in a chilling tone. "But the life they steal doesn't last long. At dawn, they are drawn back to their graves to sleep, and when they wake they are Creepers, looking for another soul to feed on!"

"What happens to the people whose souls they take?" quivered LB, clinging onto Snoddy.

"They too become Creepers," replied Scoutt, stretching out his hands and wiggling his fingers imitating a Creeper.

LB gulped. "Well, I guess we'd better call it a night

then," he said, and set off rapidly back down the hill.

"Not so fast, LB," said Scoutt grabbing hold of his shoulder.

"It'll take four of us to carry the Gammell Roots back to the boat when we get them."

"I've taken a real dislike to Gammell Roots recently," announced LB. "I much prefer Tweezel Berries. Anyone for Devil's Maze?" he continued, now quivering in his shoes.

"Stop shaking," said Scoutt. "I have an idea. Why don't you stay here outside the cemetery gates on lookout, while the three of us go back through the cemetery to get to the Gammell Roots?"

"That's a brilliant idea," chirped LB, a look of relief spreading across his face.

"Oh great," thought Thumble Tumble, still hiding in the shadows. "Now I'm going to have to follow these crazy pixies all the way through the cemetery. I just hope my Return to Grave spell works on *all* the Creepers."

Chapter 4

Boat Trip to Nowhere

Blade opened his eyes to see his own blurred reflection staring back at him. His head was pounding from being bounced around inside his glass prison.

He could see Mogdred hovering a few inches off the ground ahead of Ugg and Ogg. Just by the wave of a finger, she was ripping tree after tree out by its roots, making a rough path through the thick foliage.

"Be careful with that jar!" she screeched at Ugg. "We need him alive."

"Yes... for now," chuckled Ugg, licking his lips as he peered into the jar at the bewildered Blade.

Every second minute, Blade was thrown to the base of the jar as it bumped over a huge stone, or smashed off the side as it tilted up against a log or other obstacle.

After Blade had suffered a full hour of this treatment, Ugg deposited the jar on the ground and turned his attention to scoffing a handful of slugs.

Blade got to his feet and flew with all his might towards

the lid, then went hurtling straight back down.

"It's hopeless," he sighed.

As he lay on his back feeling utterly defeated, he suddenly noticed that the lid was the sort that twisted off. Gathering all his remaining strength, he fluttered up until he could touch its underside. He tried to turn the lid, but his hands just slipped across it.

"Codswallop!" he shouted.

Then he spat a huge dollop of sap onto each hand.

"That should do it," he thought. He stuck both hands onto the underside of the lid with the sticky saliva sap and fluttered as fast as he could in a clockwise direction. All that happened was his body wrapped itself around his arms. He untangled himself and tried fluttering anti-clockwise.

The lid began to move! Unfortunately, before it had made a full turn, Ugg finished stuffing the last of the slugs into his mouth and abruptly started trailing the jar along again.

The journey was now so bumpy that Blade could not even flutter up to the lid. Ugg was continually bashing the jar into something, sending Blade hurtling around inside.

"Brilliant," Blade muttered hopelessly to himself.

Just then, he noticed something quite advantageous: with every bump, the lid was loosening. Sure enough, little by little, the lid slowly twisted itself open.

Oblivious to what was happening, Ugg and Ogg continued following Mogdred until they left the forest and found themselves on the seashore.

"You two use that to get to the Holy Isle," Mogdred told them, pointing her long black finger towards a dilapidated rowing boat.

"I'll meet you on the other side."

With that, she swirled into a puff of black ash and disappeared.

Ugg placed the glass jar on the sand and limped across to help Ogg push the rowing boat into the water.

"I hope we don't come across any of those crazed Thistle Pixies," huffed Ogg as they hauled the boat along the shore.

"Don't worry," said Ugg, "Mogdred will take care of them. You know how much she loves Thistle Pixies… especially smothered in gravy!"

"OK, but remember what they did to your foot," Ogg said, still worried.

"How can I forget," Ugg bellowed. "I'm reminded of it every time I take a step. Why else do you think I agreed to help Mogdred?"

"Because you're afraid of her?" Ogg hazarded.

"Well, that too… but mainly because I want to see those pixies devoured!" Ugg clenched his fists. "Come on, we'd better hurry up. If we keep Mogdred waiting, the only thing to be devoured will be us."

The Tree Trolls eventually managed to haul the boat out into the water. They jumped in and Ugg grabbed the single oar, while Ogg spread out his hand in the shape of a paddle. They propelled themselves out from the shoreline then began to row back and forth. After rowing for twenty minutes they arrived at land.

"That was quick," said Ugg smugly.

"But… isn't this the same place we started?" asked Ogg, blinking rapidly.

"What makes you say that?" demanded Ugg.

"The jar," Ogg said, pointing to an empty jar rolling

along the beach. "It looks just like the one we had the Flower Nymph in."

"*Oh no!*" screamed Ugg. "*Mogdred will kill us!*"

He clambered out of the rowing boat and waded towards the shore.

Blade was fluttering off through the undergrowth as fast as his eight tiny wings could carry him.

He could hear Ugg screaming, "Where are you?" as he tore through the forest, kicking up the undergrowth with his good foot, sending leaves and dirt flying into the air.

"I can smell you," Ugg bawled as he gained on Blade.

Blade could feel tremors in the ground as Ugg ploughed towards him, following the sweet smell of roses. Blade was overwhelmed with despair, for the faster he fluttered his wings in his effort to escape, the stronger the tell-tale scent grew.

He changed his tactics and crawled under an elm leaf, where he lay motionless as Ugg pounded past a short distance to his left.

No longer able to smell the aroma of rosebuds, Ugg was unable continue tracking the tiny Flower Nymph. If he had thought about it, he might have waited in case the scent came back, but that was beyond him. Instead, he stormed off into the forest, shouting and wailing as he went.

Ugg's yells faded into the distance before Blade crept out from under the leaf. Rather than fluttering, he tiptoed through the undergrowth, fearful of the Tree Troll getting a whiff of his scent again.

Up ahead, he could see a pond. In the gentle breeze, the surface of the water was flickering in the moonlight.

The pond was getting closer with every step… *much*

closer!

"That's strange," Blade thought, suddenly finding that he was almost standing in the water. Then a huge round object came hurtling towards him. By the time he managed to turn, it was too late.

The lid of the jar was once more sealed tight shut.

The jar had acted like a magnifying glass, making the pond seem much closer than it really was, and so once more entrapping Blade."Tut, tut," grinned Mogdred, tapping the side of his glass prison with her nails.

She glanced up as Ugg came limping through the trees.

"Take this," she snapped, thrusting the jar into his branch-like hands, "and do *not* lose him again. *Or I will devour you!"* she added in a spine-chilling hiss. "See you later, my pretty," she shrieked at Blade.

Then once again Mogdred disappeared in a puff of ash.

Chapter 5

Rise of the Creepers

Scoutt adjusted his black gnome hat as he walked back through the gates into Blakk Cemetery. Rocky and Snoddy paused for a few seconds. They looked over at one another, shrugged their shoulders, then followed. The three Thistle Pixies hadn't ventured far when they heard LB screaming. They turned on their heels and ran back to the entrance gates, where they'd left him.

"Are you OK? What happened?" panted Scoutt, holding his sides, bent double, trying to catch his breath.

"Everything is A-OK," LB answered, saluting Scoutt as though he was a colonel in the army. "I was just checking you could hear me in case of an emergency, *sir*," he continued in a military tone.

"Are you mad?" gasped Scoutt, lunging forward with every intention of choking LB. Snoddy and Rocky pulled him back.

"We don't have time for you to strangle him," said Snoddy, "but if you do that again..." he said, leaning in as though about to whisper into LB's ear.

"I'LL THROTTLE YOU MYSELF," he yelled.

LB almost jumped out of his skin.

"Sorry, guys," he mumbled sheepishly.

Scoutt, Snoddy and Rocky headed back into the cemetery. After a few steps, Scoutt launched himself belly-first onto the ground and began slinking along the path. Snoddy and Rocky followed suit. LB watched his friends disappear into the fog that was now winding its way amongst the graves.

Thumble Tumble's ears were still buzzing from LB's high-pitched screams, which had sent her tumbling to the ground. As she picked herself up, she noticed a dank chill in the air and realised that the cemetery was swiftly being engulfed in a blanket of dense grey fog. Within seconds, she could barely see her hands out in front of her, never mind the Thistle Pixies.

"Oh no!" she gasped, and ran blindly forward.

Meanwhile, Scoutt was gliding along the path like an eel slipping through water. Snoddy and Rocky were less graceful as they dragged themselves along side by side.

Strange-looking figures could be seen rising up from the tombs as they progressed through the cemetery in stealth-mode between the gravestones.

"I'm not sure this was such a great idea," Rocky whispered as more and more of the creatures clambered out of their crypts.

"Really?" Snoddy replied sarcastically.

"Be quiet, you two," Scoutt said in a hushed tone. "They're dead, not deaf!"

Rocky couldn't stop himself from bursting out laughing.

"Dead, not deaf," he chortled, lying on his back and stomping his feet on the ground.

The hysteria seemed to be contagious, for Snoddy collapsed on the ground beside Rocky, laughing uncontrollably.

By the time the pair had managed to stop laughing, a mob of Creepers were hovering over them.

One of the Creepers stretched its hand towards Snoddy. As the creature leaned towards him, Snoddy felt an excruciating pain in his head. He felt the top of his head – where he found Scoutt's hand, firmly clenched around his massive tuft of hair.

Scoutt could finally see the way out and he started racing towards the gates, pulling Rocky and Snoddy by their hair behind him.

Another Creeper lunged forward and this time managed to catch hold of Snoddy's right foot. Snoddy could feel his body stretching between Scoutt's firm grip and the Creeper's cold grasp. He kicked his leg frantically, shaking his ankle, then shot forward as his right shoe went flying off into the cemetery, taking half a dozen Creepers with it.

Snoddy scrambled to his feet.

"Your lucky shoe!" shouted Scoutt, as he watched

Snoddy's shoe disappear into the fog.

"Don't worry about that," Snoddy shouted back as he lifted Rocky's feet off the ground. The two pixies sprinted towards the gate, carrying Rocky's body like a stretcher between them.

"The gate looks closed!" Scoutt gasped over his shoulder to Snoddy.

"Keep running," squealed Snoddy.

The snarling Creepers were right behind him.

Scoutt ran straight into the gate, then rebounded, face-first, onto the ground, dropping Rocky with a thud.

Snoddy tripped over their bodies and went flying through the air towards the gates, which he hit dead-centre with the top of his skull. Even that didn't budge them. The Thistle Pixies sat up and started pushing themselves along the ground with their backs to the gates. The row of Creepers gathered in front of them began to advance on their prey, moaning as they readied themselves to take their rewards.

Scoutt put an arm around each of his friends. "Close your eyes," he whispered.

"Can they not get us with our eyes closed?" Rocky asked hopefully.

"I'm afraid they can," replied Scoutt, his head bowed. "But at least you won't need to see anything."

The three friends huddled together and closed their eyes.

Scoutt felt his chest tighten and a burning sensation travelled from the tip of his toes up through his body to his head. Then he had the strangest feeling. It was as though he was floating in the air!

The Creepers' growls dissolved into silence and

gradually Scoutt's body floated back down to earth. As he landed he thought he could feel the Creepers grabbing at him again.

"Scoutt! Scoutt!" they were calling out. "*Open your eyes.*"

Scoutt was almost ready to give in to his fate when he realised that their voices sounded familiar.

He opened his eyes and was hugely relieved to see his friends leaning over him.

"Are you alright?" asked Snoddy.

I think so," said Scoutt, still dazed. "How did we escape?"

"We don't know," answered Rocky, equally bewildered. "We closed our eyes just as you told us to, and the next thing we knew we were lying here on the ground beside you... *outside the cemetery!*" He spoke the last three words in a crescendo to emphasise the importance of their new location, then said, "Now let's get out of here!"

Thumble Tumble had waited until she was sure the Thistle Pixies had gone before she waved her wand. "Revaporatio!" she said, as she twirled it around her invisible body. A faint image of her silhouette gradually began to appear. It flickered in and out of transparency several times before forming into a solid figure.

Thumble Tumble sat down on the grass outside the cemetery walls and breathed a huge sigh of relief that she'd actually managed to save the Thistle Pixies from the Creepers – just in the nick of time!

As soon as the Thistle Pixies closed their eyes, she had blasted them with a Transporting Spell, which had lifted the Thistle Pixies up out of the clutches of the Creepers and over the wall to safety.

She was recounting in her head just how well she had executed the complex transporting spell, when she noticed a small plaque attached to the wall with a couple of rusty nails. On it was an arrow pointing left. Below the arrow there was writing – words that appeared to be etched in blood...

Miss Malovent's Garden

"Tell me they're not heading for Miss Malovent's Garden," Thumble Tumble groaned to herself.

She leapt to her feet and sprinted off in the direction of the arrow.

Chapter 6

What Lies Beneath

Blade sat helplessly in the jar and watched as Ugg and Ogg once more pushed the dilapidated boat into the water. This time, they didn't forget to load their precious cargo!

The trolls had found an oar lying on the sand, but even with two oars, they still managed to row in a circle for ten minutes before finally working out how to paddle in a straight line and commence their voyage to the Holy Isle .

As they journeyed away from shore, the calm sea gleamed in brilliant shades of blue in the moonlight. The little rowing boat bobbed along gently until, about a mile out from the Holy Isle, hordes of golden flying fish started shooting out of the water, moonbeams bouncing off their tiny fins.

"Aw, they look so nice," said Ogg.

"Yes, nice and juicy," replied Ugg, slobbering over the side of the boat.

The trolls exchanged a malicious grin, before reaching out and grabbing at the golden fish as they surged out of the water. The trolls lunged further and further out over the sides of the boat in an effort to catch the tasty fish. Its gentle swaying became a furious rocking motion, until it capsized, throwing Ugg and Ogg into the swirling waves.

Ugg began shrieking at the top of his voice. "Help, help... I can't swim," he bawled.

"Do shut up," Ogg shouted back at him. "You're made of wood. You don't need to swim – you'll float!"

"Oh, that's right," replied Ugg, composing himself. "I completely forgot."

The Tree Trolls splashed around, vainly attempting to reach the boat, which was now upside down and floating out to sea on the strong current.

Eventually, Ugg managed to grab a hold of Ogg's foot and throw him so that Ogg could get hold of the side of the boat. He managed to tip it back over and drag himself on board.

"Get the jar," he shouted to Ugg, pointing at Blade's glass prison.

Ugg looked round to see the jar bobbing in the sea just a few feet away from him, with their Flower Nymph prisoner looking out in dismay.

"I'm not going over there," Ugg called back to Ogg. "The jar's in the Lurgie!"

The jar had drifted from the shimmering blue waters into a darkly turbulent patch that resembled a brown swamp.

"It's only at the edge of the Lurgie," Ogg hollered back. "The serpents never venture near the edge of the Lurgie," he lied.

"I don't care," said Ugg, folding his arms as he floated in the water. "I'm not taking *any* chances. If the serpents get a hold of me they'll drag me to a watery grave at the bottom of the sea – wood or not!"

"If you don't get that jar, Mogdred will make a watery grave look like a day in a sweet shop," Ogg retorted.

Reluctantly, Ugg paddled off. He could see Blade jumping up and down in a frenzy, his hands cupped around his mouth, shouting something.

"That stupid Flower Nymph," he thought. "Doesn't he know I can't hear him?"

Blade could see the serpent swimming towards him.

"Hurry up, you moron," he yelled towards Ugg.

The serpent's claws started to fan open, ready to grasp their prize.

One of the monster's claws tipped the bottom of the jar, but it was too late. Ugg was already fishing the jar out of the murky water, using his branch-like fingers as a net.

"I'll take that," he said to the serpent, with an air of satisfaction.

The serpent retracted its claws and headed back into the depths of the Lurgie.

"I showed him!" Ugg boasted as he threw the jar into the boat. He then began pulling himself onto the boat as he continued bragging. "That's right, MR SERPENT, you're not *that* scary. You're lucky I'm in a good mood, or else I'd have… *Arrghhhh,*" he screamed, clenching on to the side of the boat as the serpent sank his claws deep into his stump.

Ogg had been so busy listening to Ugg boasting about how he'd foiled the serpent, that he hadn't noticed them drifting back into the Lurgie.

The powerfully muscled monster was at least twenty feet long. It looked like a giant black eel, except for the fin that ran along its back, laced with razor-sharp claws.

"It's too strong," Ogg cried. "You'll need to let go!"

"No way," Ugg screamed back, tightening his grip on the side of the boat, which was heaving from side to side as the serpent yanked on his leg. The jar containing Blade suddenly shattered against the port side of the boat.

"Chop off his leg!" Blade roared up at Ogg.

"Why would I do that?" Ogg asked, looking confused.

"OMG," cried Blade. "Just do it, or we'll all die!"

Ogg didn't even bother to try to work out what 'OMG' meant. He just pulled out the axe from the small toolbox on the boat and chopped off Ugg's leg, a few inches above his stump.

As soon as Ugg had crawled on board, Ogg frantically rowed away from the Lurgie. He didn't say a single word to his brother for the remainder of the journey.

When Ugg eventually recovered from his ordeal, he tied up Blade, using some twine from his little finger, all the while mumbling to himself, "Oh what's a little bit of twine, *or half your leg for that matter!*"

"I'm so sorry," Ogg grovelled. "It was the only way. It wasn't me, it was the Flower Nymph – he *made* me do it! And anyway, it's not like I cut off your foot – it was already a stump!"

Chapter 7

Miss Malovent

"It's this way," Scoutt said confidently, pointing in the direction indicated by the arrow.

"Who is Miss Malovent?" asked Rocky.

"Miss Malovent is a very talented shape shifter who is famous for growing the most amazing herbs and plants," replied Scoutt.

"I've never heard of a shape shifter before," Rocky said inquisitively.

"A shape shifter is a witch that can take any shape she wants," explained Scoutt. "Unfortunately, Miss Malovent is also renowned for something other than her wonderful legumes."

"Huh?" said Rocky creasing his nose.

"Vegetables!" Snoddy interjected. "Legumes are vegetables." He then turned back to Scoutt to hear more about Miss Malovent.

Scoutt continued speaking in a low voice. "She is also famed for her evil temper… and she does NOT like people in her garden. Especially pixies who are there to steal her Gammell Roots!"

"Ah, so that's why we're here," said Rocky, as the penny finally dropped. He had been wondering why they had chosen to cut through Blakk Cemetery.

He now remembered that the only way into the enchanted garden was via Blakk Cemetery. The witch who owned the garden had located it there precisely because no one in their right mind would venture into the cemetery (unless already dead, of course!).

"But I don't understand why we had to go into the cemetery at midnight," he continued, still looking dumbfounded, "especially as that's when the Creepy Creepers come out to play."

"The Gammell Roots only ripen at midnight for one hour," replied Scoutt. "So, in order to harvest them, we had to get here right after midnight. I just hope Miss Malovent is asleep. One encounter with her is supposed to be ten times worse than coming face to face with a whole gang of Creepers." He gulped, then recommenced his recce of the gardens. "The coast is clear," he whispered, as he trod across the lawn towards the plant beds, which were full of brightly coloured plants that shimmered in the moonlight.

In front of the Thistle Pixies, a line of Spider Plants seemed to be tilting their jaggy pincers towards them. Each Spider Plant had eight long thin leaves covered in tiny hairs, giving the appearance of a tarantula's legs. The two jagged leaves that acted as pincers were situated at the top of the stem, along with hundreds of tiny berry-like eyes.

"Be careful," Scoutt called out, grabbing hold of Snoddy, who was bending down for a better look. "Those

38

pincers are deadly!"

Snoddy sprung back just as one of the Spider Plants whooshed its pincer straight past his head.

"Phew, and they are also pretty sneaky," Scoutt added, wiping his hand across his brow.

The three Thistle Pixies resumed tiptoeing through the garden, being careful not to touch any of the plants as Miss Malovent watched on through one hundred beady eyes, disguised as the Spider Plant who'd just missed Snoddy.

"The Gammell Roots are right at the back of the garden," said Scoutt, "just beyond that cage."

"Aren't those Tweezel Berry Bushes?" asked Snoddy, looking in at the bushes pacing up and down inside the huge domed cage.

"That they are," replied Scoutt.

"I thought Tweezel Berry Bushes remained inside Devil's Maze," quizzed Snoddy.

"They usually do," said Scoutt. "But Miss Malovent wanted *every* species of plant for her garden, so she trapped those poor Tweezel Berry Bushes and now keeps them locked up in that giant cage so they can't escape."

"She's a nasty piece of work then!" exclaimed Snoddy, shaking his head.

"I'll show you *nasty,*" Miss Malovent muttered to herself as she fluttered near them, now masquerading as a beautiful orange butterfly.

The pretty butterfly started twirling and twisting in the breeze. It shot past the three Thistle Pixies and flew towards the Devouring Daffs.

"Watch out," Rocky shouted, running towards the butterfly, which was now hovering almost inside the wide-open jaws on an eagerly awaiting Daff.

"No, *you* watch out," hollered Snoddy, and rugby-tackled Rocky to the ground.

Just as the two pixies landed on the dirt, the Devouring Daff snapped its jaws shut with the butterfly still inside.

"That could have been you," cried Snoddy, nodding over to the Daff, which was licking its lips is satisfaction.

"Can you please, *please* be a bit more careful. Every plant in here is extremely dangerous... and most them haven't been fed yet."

As soon as the Thistle Pixies had moved on to the next row of plants, Miss Malovent pushed out her wings and transmuted into her true form, exploding the Devouring Daff's head into a thousand tiny fragments. At her full height, she was almost six feet tall. She had long, straight orange hair, and was wearing an orange chiffon dress that floated in the breeze as she walked. She had a pretty face, which was unusual for an evil witch. Although, no one actually knew for sure if this was her real face, or just another one of her disguises.

The rest of the Devouring Daffs cowered into small buds as Miss Malovent tramped over them on her way to the Gammell Roots.

By the time Thumble Tumble caught up with them, Scoutt had his hands wrapped around a massive Gammell Root. Each of these plants was about half the size of the pixies. They were round in shape and covered with a thick, black, prickly rind. Only the top half of the fruit was on the surface with the bottom half firmly stuck below the ground.

"Heave," Scoutt shouted out, as he tugged on the plant. But nothing was happening! The Gammell Root stood rigid in the ground.

"You two grab onto my waist and we'll try pulling together," he instructed Rocky and Snoddy.

"One, two, heave!" he bellowed. The Gammell Root shot out of the ground and rolled over Scoutt's foot.

They repeated the exercise two more times, this time pushing the Gammell Roots to avoid any further damage to Scoutt's precious foot, which was way more important than the Gammell Roots.

"Lucky it wasn't your right foot," sighed Rocky.

"It was," replied Scoutt, now sitting on the ground nursing his swollen foot. He lay back on the grass to give his sore foot a well-deserved rest. The garden seemed so peaceful now. Under the stars glowing in the night sky, he was just about to drift off to sleep when he heard a rustling sound. He nudged the others and all three Thistle Pixies silently rose to their feet with their spears aimed in the direction of the noise.

"Hi guys," boomed LB, marching out from the grass.

"How on earth did you get here?" gasped Scoutt, lowering his spear.

"I found a shortcut," exclaimed LB, with a mischievous grin.

"That's weird," thought Thumble Tumble. "He didn't strike me as the adventurous type!"

"It's over here," LB said excitedly. "Quick, come on."

"Hold on," said Scoutt.

LB shot him a dark glance.

"Hey, no need to be so grumpy," smiled Scoutt. "We've just got to get the Gammell Roots first."

Scoutt, Rocky and Snoddy each took up their positions behind their respective fruits and began rolling them towards LB, who promptly turned on his heels and broke into a little jog.

"I knew it," thought Thumble Tumble, noticing a little piece of orange chiffon dangling off the hem of LB's kilt.

"Revealio!" she shouted, pointing her wand towards LB.

"Who said that?" Rocky, looked around for the owner of the mysterious voice.

"Did you hear that?" he called to the others.

But Snoddy and Scoutt weren't interested in finding the source of the voice. They were too busy watching the transformation taking place in front of their eyes.

"I said didn't you hea—" As he turned, Rocky stopped mid-sentence, stunned to see LB's legs stretch up to armpits. LB's whole body elongated up to six feet and his hair changed from purple to orange.

The apparition began spinning on the spot, and when it came to a halt, LB had morphed into a woman wearing an orange chiffon dress.

"Good evening," said Miss Malovent, smiling graciously as she moved towards them.

"Stay where you are," commanded Scoutt, his spear pointed directly at her chest. The other Thistle Pixies surrounded their 'hostess', their spears also poised ready to attack.

Miss Malovent's smile distorted into a grimace and she began to transform again.

Her eyes and hair turned jet black, as did her dress, which was now changing from flowing chiffon into a deathly cloak.

"She's changing into a Mantigh," screamed Scoutt.

"Use your screech," Thumble Tumble shouted, still in her invisible state. "Now, before the change is complete!"

The Thistle Pixies opened their mouths and in unison let loose a screech so loud, no witch could survive it!

Miss Malovent's head started to swell from the force of the piercing screech. Her face blew up like a balloon, before whooshing across the garden, dragging her partially mutated body with it. She finally landed in the bed of Devouring Daffs before exploding into a giant puff of orange smoke.

"Do you think she's dead?" asked Snoddy.

"I think so," replied Scoutt. "But I don't want to hang around here to find out. Come on, let's go."

Snoddy followed Scoutt towards the centre of the garden, pushing his Gammell Root.

Rocky waited behind for a few moments, still trying

to work out where the mysterious voice that saved them had come from.

He patted the ground all around where he'd been standing, feeling for an invisible body, but there was nothing to be found.

Eventually, he gave up and started pushing his Gammell Root towards the others.

"What about the Tweezel Berry Bushes?" Snoddy said anxiously, as they passed the huge cage imprisoning the helpless bushes.

"Ok, we'll help them," said Scoutt. "But we need to be quick if we want to get back through Blakk Cemetery before the Creepers wake up again."

Chapter 8

The Accidental Chop

The sun was rising on the horizon when Ugg and Ogg arrived at the Holy Isle.

As instructed, they pulled the row boat across the sand and hid it in a patch of long grass near where they had landed.

Ugg spoke for the first time in hours.

"We've to follow the shoreline," he said sharply. He picked up Blade who was still wrapped in twine and started making his way along the shore in a westerly direction.

"Where's Mogdred?" asked Ogg.

Ugg completely ignored him and continued pacing along the shore.

"I asked you a question," Ogg shouted angrily. "I know you're mad at me but it really wasn't my fault. *It was that Flower Nymph*," he shrieked, prodding Blade on the ribs with his long twiggy fingers.

"You know fine well I would never have come up with

that idea on my own."

"Or any idea!" Ugg replied with a nasty smirk. "Mogdred won't arrive until nightfall," he continued, answering Ogg's previous question.

"Oh great, we're stuck here on a tiny island inhabited by a bunch of wild Thistle Pixies, and the witch who sent us hasn't even arrived yet," moaned Ogg. "What happens if we bump into any pixies before she gets here?"

Ugg had a flashback to his last encounter with the Thistle Pixies. He'd been ordered by the Night Witches to go to the Holy Isle to spy on the Buddhists, the keepers of the Cauldron of Undry. His mission was to find out where the hidden entrance to the Buddhists Temple was so that Mogdred could steal the magical cauldron.

Ugg had spent weeks lying on his belly, concealed by the undergrowth without so much as seeing a Buddhist. Then one day he overheard a group of Thistle Pixies discussing how they were going to fell some trees to get firewood for the Buddhists.

"Great," thought Ugg. "I'll pretend to be a tree and the pixies will take me straight to the Buddhists Temple!"

Ugg snuck through the undergrowth, beating the Thistle Pixies to a small area of woodland where he knew they chopped down trees.

He stood against an old tree and waited. His body blended in so well, he was almost invisible.

When the Thistle Pixies arrived, they started marking some of the trees with big red crosses.

"This old tree looks pretty grim," one said, painting a big red cross on Ugg's shin.

"Huh, I can't look that grim if you're painting a kiss on me," thought Ugg.

A split second later, the Thistle Pixie pulled out an axe, shouted 'timber' and chopped off Ugg's foot.

"*Arrghh!*" Ugg screamed right into Ogg's face as he came hurtling back to reality.

The shriek gave Ogg such a fright that he almost jumped out of his bark.

"All right, I get the picture," Ogg squealed when he'd unruffled his bark. "We DO NOT want to bump into any Thistle Pixies!"

"Correct answer," Ugg snapped, then resumed tramping along the beach towards his rendezvous point with Mogdred.

Chapter 9

The Eagalach Cup

Thumble Tumble opened her eyes fully expecting to see her body lying several feet away from her head, somewhere inside Miss Malovent's garden. She was pleasantly surprised when the first thing she saw was a pair of shoes loosely tied to her feet, which were still perfectly attached to the rest of her body.

"The Transporting Spell must have worked again," she thought to herself in disbelief as she gazed around at her new surroundings.

Thumble Tumble had blasted herself with the spell a millisecond before the Thistle Pixies discharged their head-busting screech. But the reason for her disbelief was not the close timing of her escape. It was because she had managed to get the Transporting Spell to work.

Thumble Tumble had never managed to execute the spell before, and now she'd done it twice in one night! Each time she had previously attempted to move an object, it either hadn't budged at all, or ended up in several pieces, all having been transported to different locations. Her spell book itself had separated into twenty pages, each ending up on a different bush in the back garden, where she'd been practising her Protective Virtuosities… and she'd never dared use the spell on a person before.

Thumble Tumble didn't know how long she'd been unconscious, but it must have been several hours, as the sun was now high in the sky.

She was surrounded by ice-cold air, lying on a blanket of snow that glistened in the sunlight. She would have frozen for sure if it hadn't been for her bright red cloak, which thankfully did exactly what it said on the label:

This cloak will keep you cool when it's hot, warm when it's cold and dry when it's wet. Love Auntie Isla x.

Thumble Tumble felt a familiarity about this barren landscape. She spotted a glossy red door in the distance and a huge smile spread across her face. When she reached the door, she took particular care to avoid the large silver knocker that she knew would send a tornado of sound through the inside of the crooked white house. Instead, she took out her wand and gently tapped the door three times.

After a few moments Thumble Tumble could hear the grumpy tones of her dear friend, McCools.

"Alright, alright, I'm coming," he grouched. Who's there?" he demanded from behind the door.

"It's me," replied Thumble Tumble, giggling.

"How do I know it's you?"

Despite McCools' grouchy tone, the door swung open and a ball of orange fur with two big purple eyes thrust its bony arms around her, giving the biggest hug ever.

"To what do I owe this unexpected pleasure?" asked the three-legged Haggis as he led Thumble Tumble in out of the cold. McCools took Thumble Tumble's cloak and hung it up on a peg beside the door. He then ushered her into the lounge and sat her in front of the cosy fire.

"Tea?" he enquired.

"Yes please," replied Thumble Tumble, realising she had not eaten for a whole day. She was ravenous.

McCools prepared a pot of thistle tea, which he poured into two large mugs. He handed one mug to Thumble Tumble along with a plate piled high with dandelion cookies. The pair of them then tucked in to the cookies whilst drinking their tea, and Thumble Tumble told McCools all about her extraordinary evening with the Thistle Pixies and their quest for Gammell Roots.

When she'd finished telling her story McCools burst into a fit of laughter.

"Ah, those crazy Thistle Pixies. They'll do just about anything when it comes to the Eagalach Cup."

"The Eagalach Cup? What's that?" Thumble Tumble asked.

"It's a tournament played by all of the Pixie clans," explained McCools. "Every four years the clans gather to play a game called Eagalach. Each team plays against another and the winning teams go through to the next round. Eventually there are only two teams left. This is called 'the final', and the winner of this match takes the Eagalach Cup. This year is very special for the Thistle Pixies, as it's the first time they have been in the final."

"Wow, that is exciting," gasped Thumble Tumble. "Who are they playing against?"

"That's the bad news. They are playing against the reigning champions – the Cornflower Pixies, undefeated for the past twelve years."

"Sorry if I sound a bit silly, but what's this got to do with Gammell Roots?" Thumble Tumble wondered.

"Well, as you know the Thistle Pixies are a bit feisty. These little guys are so excited about being in the Eagalach Cup Final, they've already started preparing their celebratory feast."

"Let me guess," said Thumble Tumble. "They feast on Gammell Roots, don't they? No wonder they're referred to as 'crazy' Thistle Pixies."

McCools nodded. "Who else would cut through Blakk Cemetery at midnight, dodging soul-sucking Creepers, then evading the clutches of Miss Malevolent, just to get their hands on some Gammell Roots?"

"I'd love to see the Eagalach Cup Final. Do you think the Thistle Pixies would let us watch it?" Thumble Tumble said eagerly.

"Not a chance," McCools replied, shaking his head. "The Thistle Pixies are very protective of the Eagalach Cup. Only pixies are allowed in the stadium during the Cup Final."

"Why so protective?" asked Thumble Tumble.

"Like most pixie cups, the Eagalach Cup has magical powers," replied McCools. "However, unlike any of the other pixie cups, the Eagalach Cup has the power of destruction. In the wrong hands, the Eagalach Cup could be deadly! So, the pixies are taking no chances… they cannot allow the cup to fall into Mogdred's possession."

"Oh," said Thumble Tumble glumly. "Couldn't we just sneak in?" she persisted, with a cheeky grin.

"Nope," McCools answered abruptly. "As an extra layer of defence, the pixies are preventing entry to the Holy Isle for all witches, good and evil. The tiny island is protected by a magical barrier that emanates from the unicorns who live deep within the caves that lie along the western shore. The unicorns are enchanted and cannot be killed, not even by dark magic. So you see, it really is impossible for you to watch the Eagalach Cup Final."

"What's so special about the magical barrier? I could just transport right through it," Thumble Tumble responded, with a hint of arrogance.

McCools looked straight into her eyes and his voice took on an intensely serious tone. "The barrier is very powerful, Thumble Tumble. If you so much as brush against it, you'll be frazzled instantly – *do you understand?"* Thumble Tumble nodded.

McCools lightened up slightly. "And I don't fancy explaining to your aunts how you ended up as 'Toast à la Thumble! Besides, the game of Eagalach is very complicated, and very few people other than pixies understand the rules. In fact, half the pixies don't even understand the rules! So, you probably wouldn't be able to follow the game, even if you could see it."

"Do you know the rules?" she asked.

"Vaguely," replied McCools. "From what I understand there are eleven players on each team. Five 'runners' who play on the pitch running after the ball. Their job is to kick the ball into the other team's net. This is pretty difficult though, as the ball has legs, and so it runs away."

"I would run away too if someone tried to kick me," Thumble Tumble gasped.

"No need to be alarmed," McCools continued. "The balls can't feel anything. They are specially trained from the moment they are created to seek the net. So as soon as they see a net, they run straight towards it. If the ball runs into the other team's net, you score one point. If you manage to kick it into the other team's net, you score three points."

"What about the other players?" quizzed Thumble Tumble. "You said there were eleven!"

"Oh, that's right," said McCools. "Each team also has a 'keeper' whose role is to prevent the ball from entering the net, and the other five players are 'clinchers'. These guys are very agile and they all have enormous hands. They are not on the pitch, instead they are positioned along the side-lines to catch the ball if it leaves the pitch. When they catch the ball, they throw it back onto the pitch in the direction of the opposing team's net. This is called a 'fluky'. The team with the most points after ninety minutes wins the game."

Chapter 10

The Conjuring

Blade was covered in bumps and bruises by the time they arrived at their destination. His eight tiny wings were tattered and torn from bouncing off the shoreline as Ugg dragged his little torso along.

"You took your time," a woman's voice rang out from the bushes. "Be careful with him!" she shouted as Ugg dropped Blade's battered body onto the ground. She emerged to reveal a beautiful female Deer Folk with long flowing purple hair.

"He's no use to us dead!" she snarled at the Tree Trolls.

"What are *you* doing here?" said Ugg, taken aback by Serena's presence. His last encounter with her had been when he'd snatched her sister. "Yes, and what business is it of yours what we do with *our* Flower Nymph," piped up Ogg, still desperately trying to get back on side with Ugg after chopping off a bit more of his leg!

"*Your* Flower Nymph?" Serena echoed in a tone of disdain. "That's funny, I thought he belonged to Mogdred."

"Speaking of Mogdred, where is she?" Ugg retorted.

"Once again Mogdred recruits the most stupid of creatures," Serena tutted, shrugging her shoulders.

Menacingly, Ugg and Ogg took a step towards her, their branchy fingers spread.

Serena merely bowed her head and whipped both Tree Trolls off their feet with one swoop of her antlers.

"As I was saying," she continued, unfazed, "Mogdred seems to choose creatures with below average intelligence! Last time it was a toad, now we have a couple of Tree Trolls."

"The clue is in their name gentlemen – *Night* Witches generally only come out at *night*!"

From where Blade lay on the ground, barely breathing, he watched Serena step over the Tree Trolls and trot towards him. She untied the twine that was encapsulating him.

"Open your mouth," she said softly.

Blade didn't have the strength to do anything other than follow her instructions.

To his utter astonishment, Serena produced a vial of Fairy Dew and placed a few drops onto his tongue, then she started to bandage his injured wings with rose petals.

The Tree Trolls scowled at this apparent act of kindness.

She caught at a glimpse of them gawping at her. "We also need his wings," she snapped. "If he can't flutter he's no use to Mogdred. And if that's the case, she'll have your heads on a platter, so you'd better hope the Fairy Dew does the trick!

Now, get up you two," she ordered. "We've got a lot of work to do before Mogdred arrives."

Serena placed another glass jar over Blade. "We don't want you disappearing again," she said as she carefully nudged his bandaged wings under the rim.

Blade rolled onto his side and stared through the side, watching Serena draw a strange pattern in the sand with her hooves.

She marked out a big circle, then etched two triangles inside it. She then turned to Ugg and Ogg with a nasty grin.

"Your next job is to bring me the heart of a goat," she announced.

"What?" gasped Ugg.

"A heart," Serena repeated. "You know, the thing that beats inside your chest!"

"I know what a heart is," Ugg snarled back. "Getting one was not part of the deal. We were just to capture the Flower Nymph and bring him here."

"Ah yes," Serena mused. "I'm afraid Mogdred's deals aren't always what they seem... once she has you in her evil clutches, she *never* lets you go."

"And if we refuse?" Ugg replied defiantly.

"If you don't bring me a heart, then my orders are to take *yours*!" Serena laughed wickedly, pulling out a small dagger. After brandishing it at Ugg and Ogg, she tossed it down beside Ugg's stump and resumed drawing in the sand.

She etched two further symbols: a pentagon with five stars, one on each tip, to the left of the original circle; and to its right, a hexagon. Using her front hoof, she created the image of a crescent moon in the centre of the hexagon.

Ugg reluctantly picked up the dagger, then headed inland to find a heart.

"I'm not happy about this," Ogg groaned, dawdling behind his twin.

"It's not that I mind getting the heart of a goat, I just don't want to bump into any Thistle Pixies. "

"Shh!" Ugg signalled him to be quiet. "Up ahead," he whispered, pointing to a lone goat chewing on some tasty grass a few feet in front of them.

"You go that way," he continued, directing Ogg to the far side of the goat. "I'll go this way," he added, gesturing, "And we'll trap it in between us." "Now!" Ogg yelled loudly. The startled goat immediately bolted between the two trolls, who ran straight at one another, knocking each other to the ground.

The yell had echoed right across the island, sending every animal, bird and insect for miles, fleeing in the opposite direction to the trolls.

Hours passed, as they traipsed further and further inland, without so much as spotting a fly, let alone another goat.

"We're doomed," whined Ogg. "If we don't return with a heart soon, Serena will find us and use our own hearts for Mogdred's dark spell. And if we run away... I don't want to think about what Mogdred would do to us!"

"Well if you hadn't given it such a fright, the goat wouldn't have run off," Ugg growled.

"Don't you dare blame me," Ogg blasted back at him. "It's all your fault we're on this pixie infested island in the first place. You and your lust for revenge."

"*Rhibit!*" Ugg seemed to reply.

"Did you just burp at me?" hollered Ogg.

"No, I did not," Ugg shouted back at him "*Rhibit!*"

"Yes, you did," snarled Ogg. "And you've just done it again!"

The two trolls grabbed one another by the throat and struggled until they fell to the ground.

They did not notice the frog watching them roll around the ground, holding one another in a headlock.

"This is fabulous," thought the frog to himself. 'Ringside seats at a wrestling match! The only thing that could make this experience any better would be a snack.'

Just then, he heard a delightful humming sound. "Mmm, perfect timing," he slobbered, turning around to see what flavour of snack he was about to gobble up.

But before he could release his tongue to snatch his prey, he felt an enormous weight land on his back with a force that made his eyes bulge out of their sockets like two big mushrooms. The greedy frog had been so busy looking for a bug to scoff that he hadn't noticed the interlocked, hefty trolls hurtling towards him.

By the time he realised what was happening, it was too late!

Night had fallen when Ugg and Ogg returned to find Serena pacing up and down the shoreline impatiently.

"Where have you been?" she bellowed.

"Mogdred will be furious! I just hope you managed to find a goat's heart!"

"We have what you want," smiled Ogg, holding out a heart to her in his twiggy fingers.

"Well, I can't say I'm not surprised,' Serena said with a slight quiver in her voice. "I didn't think you'd manage it." A tiny tear appeared in the corner of her eye. "Pesky flies," she snapped, and flicked the tear away with her hand.

"It was actually an acci…" Ogg stopped mid-flow as Ugg threw his hand across his mouth.

"Looks like we're not as incapable as you thought," Ugg smirked.

"No, so it would appear… even if it was by accident!" Serena conceded.

"What exactly do we need a *goat's* heart for?" Ugg quizzed her, completely ignoring her jibe about getting the heart by accident.

"Mogdred can't get through the magical barrier that protects the Holy Isle," Serena explained, "so, the only way to bring her here is to use magic… very powerful dark magic! We must conjure her from the Underworld, but in order to do that, we must pay the Lord of Darkness with the heart of a goat."

The Tree Trolls glanced at one another with a look of concern.

"You *should* be concerned," said Serena, noticing how scared the trolls looked. "Dabbling with dark magic can be *very* dangerous."

She was now thoroughly enjoying watching the trolls squirm. "That'll teach you for snatching Alfy," she thought to herself. "Place the heart in the centre symbol," she ordered Ugg, who was now looking a very pale shade of grey.

Serena picked up a handful of dirt and began to chant.
"*Oh Lord of the Darkness hear my call,*
A witch I must conjure, the most evil of all,
To you the moon and the stars I bring,
Along with this heart, as an offering."

She threw the dirt onto the symbol and took several steps back.

Mesmerised, the Tree Trolls stepped closer to get a better look.

59

They saw the ground below the centre symbol begin to move. A slight bump on the sand lifted the heart a few inches off the ground; this was followed by a massive explosion that sent dirt and sand flying up into the air.

Mogdred's body started to rise out of the ground.

The force of the explosion sent Ugg and Ogg hurtling through the air. Serena had been clever enough to step back far enough not to be affected by the blast.

By now, Mogdred's entire body had emerged from the ground. Her eyes were red with fury.

"I said the heart of a *goat!*" she shrieked at Serena.

"And that's what I told them," Serena protested, pointing at the trolls.

"It *was* the heart of a goat," Ogg said sheepishly.

"How do you explain *this* then?" Mogdred lifted her cloak to reveal a frog's leg where her left leg had been.

Chapter 11

The Bolt Ball

Gracie was sitting on a bench at the side of the training pitch, listening intently as her two team mates recounted their terrifying experience with the Creepers and Miss Malovent.

The only female member of the Thistle Pixie Eagalach team, Gracie played up front as a clincher. She could always tell where the ball was going to be next, an ability which gave her a fantastic advantage on the pitch. This unusual talent had been bestowed on her not long after she was born.

To celebrate Gracie's birth, her parents had thrown a party and invited every single Thistle Pixie in the land to take part in the wonderful celebrations.

Many brought extravagant gifts of food and drink. But one elderly couple arrived wearing tatty old cloaks and holding only a wrinkly prune in their hands.

"This is all we have," said the old lady, handing over the prune.

"Thank you for your generous gift," replied Gracie's father. "Now please come and join us."

He lavished the elderly couple with as much food as they could eat, and when they were leaving Gracie's mum handed them two massive bags stuffed to the brim with delicious delicacies.

"But all we gave you was a prune!" the elderly lady exclaimed.

"Not at all," replied Gracie's mum. "You gave us everything you had. I just hope our daughter grows up with half as much generosity as you have shown us today."

The old lady smiled, and a warm glow emanated throughout the room.

"It is you have shown great generosity today," she replied. "We would like to repay you, with one more small token,"

She produced a shiny silver bracelet from a fold in her cloak.

"No, we couldn't possibly accept such a magnificent gift," gasped Gracie's mum.

"Then Gracie shall have it," replied the old lady. She and her husband vanished into thin air and the enchanted bracelet found itself fastened on to baby Gracie's wrist.

As she got older, the magical bracelet gave Gracie the power to see into the future. By the time she was five, she could see ten seconds ahead. Now, at the age of ten, she could see a full two minutes into the future, which is more than enough when on the pitch playing Eagalach.

Gracie was only half a foot tall, and her upward-pointing purple hair had streaks of blonde twisting through it. She had huge, bright blue eyes and wore a permanent smile on her face.

"What happened next?" she gasped, as Rocky continued his story of the encounter with the Creepers and Miss Malevolent.

"She was transforming into a Mantigh when I threw my first punch!" he said dramatically.

"Actually, you were still looking for the mysterious voice when she transformed," Scoutt reminded him with a little nudge.

"Anyway," continued Rocky, willing Scoutt to be quiet, "we managed to escape her evil clutches just in time to save the Tweezel Berry Bushes."

"Save them from what?" Gracie asked excitedly.

"A fate worse than death!" Rocky replied.

"Not quite," Scoutt interjected, once again ruining Rocky's version of the story. "We did set them free, but I don't think Miss Malovent had plans to kill them."

"I'm sure being trapped in a cage, miles away from their loved ones felt like a fate worse than death to the Tweezel Berry Bushes," Gracie said diplomatically.

"Your visionary powers go way beyond just being able to see into the future," smiled Scoutt. "You are a very clever young lady, with wisdom way beyond your years," he continued, with a little wink. "Now, let's get down to business. We need to find out which ball has been selected for the final."

The team mates left the training grounds and set off for the stadium.

It was quite a long walk and Rocky continued to add details to his story, until by the time they arrived he had supposedly fought off a dozen Creepers and saved his friends, as well as the Tweezel Berry Bushes, from Miss Malovent.

They headed down a flight of stairs to the Ref's Room, where the referee stored the Eagalach balls.

Scoutt knocked on the door marked 'Ref', but there was no answer. He tried the handle, and was surprised to find the door unlocked. They decided that as the door wasn't locked, it would do no harm to pop inside.

There were no windows in the Ref's Room, which was lit by a large light suspended from the ceiling.

In the middle of the room there was a small wooden bench that had famous Eagalach players' autographs carved into it, including 'Posh Boy', the most brilliant player from the Rose Pixie Clan, and 'The Flea', the fancy-footed Ceibo Pixie Clan star. There was a display cabinet housing three whistles, one bronze, one silver and one gold. A little label in front of the bronze whistle stated: 'This whistle has served in 1,003 Eagalach games'. The silver whistle's label bore the words: 'This whistle has been used eight times – the number of times the Thistle Pixie Clan has qualified for the Eagalach Cup'. And the gold whistle's label said: 'This whistle is eagerly awaiting its first outing in an Eagalach Cup Final'.

"I bet the ref can't wait to get that around his neck," said Scoutt, awestruck by the gleaming golden whistle.

Opposite the display cabinet there was a row of four boxes, each of which had a hole cut into the top.

"That's where the Eagalach Balls are kept," whispered Gracie, pointing to the four boxes.

Four types of Eagalach Balls were set up, ready for selection. Although every Eagalach ball is trained to run into the nearest net, each one has its own unique characteristics. Knowing which ball was going to be on the pitch at the Cup Final would definitely give a team an edge over their opponents.

The 'Sonter Ball', the slowest of the Eagalach balls, is rarely used, perhaps because it is never in a hurry to get anywhere. This would be the best ball selection for the game – from the players' point of view. The 'Hare Ball', on the other hand, is extremely fast, but this little guy is prone to snoozing, so, again, not a bad choice, from a player's perspective.

The 'Scurry Ball' is extremely quick and agile, but often indecisive, and therefore not the worst option for the team.

The 'Bolt Ball', named for good reason after a lightning bolt, travels at the speed of light without hesitation, or rest – definitely a player's worst nightmare.

Gracie tiptoed towards the boxes.

"Oi, what are you lot doing in here?" came a gruff voice from the corner of the room. From under a huge pile of socks there emerged a grey-haired Thistle Pixie with a beard that went all the way down to the floor.

"Sorry, ref!" said Scoutt, taken aback. "I didn't realise you were here."

"Obviously not!" the ref grumped back. "I hope you're

not trying to steal a sneak preview of the ball."

"No, of course we're not," Gracie said hurriedly. "We just wanted to make sure you're OK. I mean… with all the preparation for the cup final, you've probably not even had lunch!"

"No, you're right, I haven't," replied the Ref, looking wistful.

"That's what we thought," said Gracie, unpacking some packages from her rucksack. "So we've brought you some pickle juice and blueberry sandwiches… I hope you like them?"

"Like them… I love them," answered the Ref, now positively perky. "It's as though you read my mind."

"She did," sniggered Scoutt in a whisper.

"Shh!" Gracie glowered at him as she unwrapped the blueberry sandwiches and stacked them onto a plate.

The ref immediately started tucking into the sandwiches. Gracie poured a bag of pickles into a jar. "Where's your pickle press?" she asked.

"Over there," he mumbled through a mouthful of bread, pointing in the direction of the four boxes.

Gracie picked up the jar of pickles and spent the next ten minutes pressing them into a smooth pickle juice.

"Here you go," she announced, handing the ref a cup full of freshly squeezed pickle juice. "Well, we'd better be on our way."

"We had?" questioned Rocky, frowning over towards the boxes.

"Yes, we had," Gracie replied sharply. "Remember, we've got a lot of training to pack in before the big game."

"Wait a minute," piped up the ref, as the three team mates rushed towards the door. They stopped in their tracks, staring back at him.

"I didn't thank you for lunch," he continued.

"Oh, no need," replied Gracie, and she resumed shoving Rocky and Scoutt in the direction of the door.

"Well, thanks anyway," the ref said. "And I hope you got what you were looking for," he added with a little laugh.

Gracie didn't stop chivvying her team mates along until they had travelled up the stairs and all the way outside the stadium.

"So?" questioned Scoutt.

"It couldn't be any worse," replied Gracie, shaking her head.

"Huh… what couldn't be any worse?" asked Rocky, still oblivious to what had just gone on.

"It's the Bolt Ball," she said.

"How do you know that?" Rocky asked, bewildered.

"When I was preparing the pickle juice, I managed to look inside the boxes. The Bolt Ball is wearing the Eagalach colours."

"But how did you know he liked pickle juice and blueberry sandwiches?" queried Scoutt. "Can you read minds as well as see into the future?" he asked excitedly.

"No," laughed Gracie. "I just followed him to the sandwich shop the other day and watched what he bought."

Gracie didn't stop laughing until they had made it all the way back to the training grounds.

Chapter 12

Box Aplenty

When she'd finished her tea and biscuits, Thumble Tumble realised she didn't have a broom to get home. McCools house was perched on a cliff on the peak of Goatfell, and the only way down was to fly or use her Transporting Spell again. And she didn't feel confident that she'd be lucky a third time using the spell.

"How am I going to get home?" she asked McCools anxiously. "My aunts will be worried sick when they realise I'm not in my bed."

"Why don't you just enchant one of my brooms and use it to fly home?" replied McCools.

"I'm not sure that's an option," she said. "I've only ever cast a Cleaning Spell on a normal broom before."

"Can't you just tweak the spell to get the broom to fly, instead of clean?" asked McCools.

"I could try," said Thumble Tumble, feeling less than confident.

McCools went to his Broom Cupboard and brought

out a standard broom with a wooden handle and twigs attached to the end with twine.

"Let's try this one," he said, handing it to Thumble Tumble.

She placed the broom on the floor, took out her wand, then stared down at the broom without speaking.

"What's wrong?" asked McCools.

"I usually say 'spick and span' for the Cleaning Spell. I'm not sure what to say for a Flying Spell."

"Don't you use spells to lift things… Why not try that?" said McCools, attempting to help.

"OK, here goes."

Thumble Tumble lifted her wand above the broom and said, "Levioso!".

The broom rose up off the ground for a few seconds, then fell back down with a huge clatter.

"You need it to stay up longer," McCools said. "Try lengthening the spell."

Thumble Tumble pointed her wand towards the broom again, and this time she shouted "Leviosioso!"

The broom slowly floated up into the air, then it flipped upside down and began sweeping the ceiling.

"It's hopeless," sighed Thumble Tumble.

"Perhaps you just need another broom?" suggested McCools.

"Sorry, another broom won't help," said Thumble Tumble, defeated.

"What if it's a witch's broom?" said McCools with a glint in his eye. He waited for the enchanted broom to finish sweeping the ceiling before grabbing hold of it and disappearing back into the Broom Cupboard.

Thumble Tumble could hear him clattering and

banging around.

"Are you OK in there?" she shouted through the closed door.

"Yes, I'm fine," McCools called back. "There's so much stuff in here it's difficult to find anything."

"Let me help," she said. She pushed the door, which swung open to reveal that the Broom Cupboard was completely empty, apart from two brooms resting neatly against the wall, and a little brown box, which McCools was peering into intently.

"Really?" questioned Thumble Tumble, throwing her hands out by her sides.

"Come over here," said McCools, directing her to look into the box.

Thumble Tumble gazed in. From the outside, the box was no bigger than a shoe box, but inside it was the size of an enormous warehouse, and it was lined, floor to ceiling, with shelves jam-packed with an array of weird objects.

"What kind of box is this?" asked Thumble Tumble, as she explored the box's intriguing contents with her eyes.

"It's called 'Box Aplenty'," McCools told her. "It's basically a magic storage box. I don't have room for all my things, so I store a few bits and bobs in here."

"A *few* things?" Thumble Tumble gulped.

"OK, quite a few things," said McCools. "Mainly things I don't use that often, or that are too dangerous to store in the house."

"Ooh, what dangerous things are there?" Thumble Tumble asked enthusiastically.

"Do you see those little trinket chests?" McCools pointed to half a dozen brightly coloured tiny chests sitting on a shelf about three-quarters of the way up one wall.

"Yes!" said Thumble Tumble, about to burst with excitement.

"They've got Rascal Goblins inside them," McCools said proudly.

"Oh…" said Thumble Tumble, looking deflated, "is that all?

"Those little critters get up to all sorts of mayhem," McCools retorted defensively.

"They're just little goblins who go around causing mischief," she said, still disappointed.

"Well, I think they're dangerous," mumbled McCools huffily. "Anyway, enough goblin chat – we need to find that witch's broom. The last time I remember seeing it, it was next to my spare scarves, right down at the bottom of the box."

"How do we get down there?" asked Thumble Tumble.

"We jump," smiled McCools, then he leapt over the side of the box.

Thumble Tumble leaned over the edge of the box. She could see McCools standing twenty feet below.

"Come on," he beckoned.

"I think I'll just climb down," she called back.

"Just jump. You won't fall… remember it's a magic box," he called back up.

"Even so, I'd rather just climb," she responded, looking nervously at the drop below.

"Fair enough," McCools replied. "I remember I was pretty scared the first time I jumped in… both my hearts were in my mouth."

"*Both* of your hearts?" quizzed Thumble Tumble.

McCools had a little chuckle to himself before he replied. "I thought everyone knew that Haggis have two hearts. One for using, and a spare for emergencies!"

He then began rummaging around the shelves looking for his witch's broom.

Thumble Tumble carefully stepped inside the box, gripping tightly to the rim. The box seemed to expand out around her.

She began climbing down, using the shelves like rungs on a ladder. She was mesmerised by the collection of things McCools had gathered over the years.

On the top shelf there was a large bronze pocket watch with the inscription: 'To McCools from your one-eyed friend, Cyclo'.

The next shelf down was covered in pens – ink pens, fountain pens, feather quills and even a pen made out of wood.

Thumble Tumble took another step down and this time she was staring into a sea of scarves. Poking out, at the very back of the shelf, was a shabby looking broomstick.

"It's here! The broom's up here!" she shouted.

"Are you sure?" asked McCools. "I could have sworn it was beside my scarves!"

"They're here too," she called back.

"Just be careful, your foot is on the shelf with the Rascal Goblins," McCools warned.

"What did you say?" asked Thumble Tumble.

Just then, she lost her balance, only for a split second, but that was enough. She felt herself losing her grip on the shelf. Throwing out her arms, she managed to grasp hold of the shelf below, but was left dangling fifteen feet off the ground. As she kicked around, trying to find a foothold, she felt her fingertips start to slip towards the edge of the shelf. At the very last second, there was a strange crunching sound as she managed to regain a precarious stance, with her feet on the shelf below..

"Phew that was close!" she gasped.

"It certainly was," said a small voice, which definitely did not belong to McCools.

Thumble Tumble looked in the direction of the voice. Along the shelf she was now holding on to stood a little green goblin the size of a mouse, with her wand in his hand.

The goblin had a bald head and pointed ears, and was wearing a tailcoat decorated in a pattern of multicoloured diamonds.

"How did you get out?" asked Thumble Tumble, startled.

"You!" the goblin yelled in her face. "Your big fat foot nearly crushed me when you trod on my chest."

He then delivered a nasty grin and stabbed Thumble Tumble on the back of her hand with the tip of her own wand.

Thumble Tumble pulled her aching hand away and as she did she went tumbling backwards towards the floor. But instead of hurtling towards the ground she fell in slow motion through the air.

She could see the little goblin climbing up the shelves towards the lid of the box as she meandered down on some sort of invisible cushion.

"I told you, you wouldn't hurt yourself," McCools said smugly as she gently landed on the ground.

Thumble Tumble was panting for air. She couldn't speak. All she could do was point up at the ceiling.

McCools glanced up just in time to see the Rascal Goblin wave at them before climbing out of the box and sealing the lid behind him.

Chapter 13

The Emerald Wood

Mogdred glowered at the two big brown frogs, deliberating whether to kill them, or turn them back into Tree Trolls.

"I think they've learned their lesson," Serena said cautiously, keenly aware that Mogdred might turn her into a frog as well. "Besides we'll need them to guard the unicorns once we capture them."

Mogdred stared at Serena with a look of disappointment, then flicked her wrist. Instantly the two frogs stopped croaking and transformed back into Ugg and Ogg.

"Thank you, my evil mistress." Ogg fell to his knees and tried to kiss Mogdred's bony hand.

"Get up, you moron," she ordered, striking him with the back of her hand. "There's no point in thanking me… I would have taken great pleasure in squashing you both. It's her you have to thank." She pointed a long black finger towards Serena.

Ogg got to his feet. "Thanks," he said disingenuously as he slunk over to his brother's side. Ugg was now even more suspicious of Serena and her acts of "kindness", even if the last one had just saved his life.

"You two, follow on in half an hour," ordered Serena.

"And in the meantime, get rid of those symbols," Mogdred interrupted, gesturing towards the sand where they had conjured her.

"But won't we need the symbols for you to leave?" Ogg continued in his grovelling tone.

"Don't concern yourself with me," roared Mogdred, remembering about her frog's leg as she hobbled along the shore. "Just do as you've been instructed before I change my mind about letting you live."

Serena shot the Tree Trolls a wicked grin before picking up the jar, with Blade still inside, and trotting along the shoreline behind Mogdred.

They hadn't travelled far when Mogdred held up her hand, indicating to Serena to stop. The route along the stony beach was extremely bumpy, and Mogdred's new leg wasn't doing her any favours, especially in the dark.

"I'm still going to kill those idiotic trolls – when I'm finished with them," she growled as she stumbled along.

"I would expect nothing less," Serena replied, with a glint in her eye.

Mogdred held her hand over a branch that was lying on the ground and uttered a spell: "Stabillious!" The branch immediately stood to attention, before morphing into a crutch. Mogdred placed it under her arm.

They walked along for another ten minutes before Mogdred put her hand up again.

"It's here," she said, pointing.

Serena stared at the wall of rock with a look of confusion on her face.

"It's hidden… obviously," Mogdred, said in a conceited tone. She scraped her wand along the cliff face in a semi-circle. "Revealio!" she commanded.

A dull green glow appeared around the contour of the semi-circle she had just drawn, then the entrance to the cave slowly swung open.

Serena walked forwards, intending to follow Mogdred into the cave.

"I must enter the cave alone," scowled Mogdred and she grabbed the glass jar out of Serena's hands.

As she seized the jar, it slipped through her long, bony fingers and smashed onto the ground.

Blade didn't waste a second. As soon as the jar shattered, he was in the air, fluttering as fast as he could towards the cave entrance.

Serena dashed after him, but Mogdred thrust out her crutch and whacked her across the stomach. The force of the blow felled Serena.

"Leave him!" Mogdred commanded.

"I don't understand," Serena groaned. "I thought we needed him!"

"Oh, we do," smirked Mogdred. "We need him to conceal my foul smell. I need to capture the unicorns, but they can smell a Night Witch from a mile away. Unless, of course, the Night Witch's rotten breath is masked by the sweet scent of a rose."

She cackled as she pulled up the hood of her cloak and followed Blade into the cave.

Blade was flying through the cave as fast as he could, but it was a labyrinth of tunnels. Each one so far had brought him right back to the where he'd started.

He fluttered through a small tunnel to his left which

seemed longer than the previous four. "Yes" he thought, as he fluttered to the end, but this too just led him to the start of the labyrinth.

"This is a nightmare!" he said aloud, fluttering back into the very first tunnel he'd tried.

This time the tunnel looked different. He noticed a green shimmer on the walls as he whizzed deeper into the cave.

He eventually emerged to find himself in a wooded clearing with an emerald-coloured river running through it.

Blade fluttered down to the ground and started to walk towards the river. As he approached the luminous green water, he rubbed his eyes in disbelief. By the fast-flowing river were two magnificent pure white unicorns, each with an ivory horn spiralling from its forehead.

As he moved towards them, the unicorns stopped drinking and turned around.

Blade had heard all about the enchanted unicorns that lived inside the Emerald Wood, and he knew the correct etiquette to be used when greeting one.

He placed one hand across his tummy, with the other around his back, and bowed all the way down until his nose touched the ground. He held this pose for five seconds before standing upright again.

The taller unicorn responded by bending his head towards Blade and tapping his front left hoof on the ground three times.

The other unicorn then stepped forward and began to lower its head. But, rather than bowing, this unicorn suddenly charged straight at Blade.

"Sleeping Death!" Mogdred's voice came booming

over his head, and with it, a snake-whip lashed out from her forefinger and bit each of the unicorns on the neck.

"No-o-o," screamed Blade, hurtling with all his might towards Mogdred.

She clipped his wings between her fingers.

"I really should be thanking you instead of killing you," she cackled.

"I mean, if you hadn't led me straight to the unicorns, I never would have been able to catch them."

"You used me!" Blade cried out as he kicked and punched in the air.

"Yes, I most certainly did," Mogdred rasped. "Unicorns can sense a Night Witch's presence from the smell of our breath. And no amount of peppermint can help!" She sniggered at her own joke. "However, there is one thing that is strong enough to mask our odour… the sweet scent of a rosebud, created by a Flower Nymph's fluttering."

"So you let me escape deliberately," Blade said miserably.

"Of course!" Mogdred cackled. "Not only did you lead me directly to the Emerald Wood, but you also disguised my fumes, enabling me to attack the unicorns at my leisure."

And with that she dropped Blade into yet another glass jar, which she concealed in a fold of her cloak.

The bright green glow of the Emerald Wood had faded to a dull grey mist, allowing Mogdred to remove the cloak from her head. She walked over to the unicorns' frozen bodies and cast a levitating spell to lift the defenceless beasts into the air, before leading them back to the entrance of the cave.

Serena was still doubled over in agony, awaiting Mogdred's return with a sense of dread. A flash of green light blasted out of the cave, illuminating the sky for a few moments, just before Mogdred appeared with the statuette bodies of the unicorns in tow.

Ugg and Ogg also arrived, having cleared away all traces of the conjuring spell (or at least, most of it).The symbols were scratched so deeply into the sand that they would have to dig them out. So, rather than wasting all their energy digging, they had simply covered over the symbols with sand.

"That'll do it," Ugg had said. The two trolls then lay down for thirty winks before heading off to meet with Mogdred.

As Mogdred left the cave, Serena noticed she was no longer limping. Her frog's leg had disappeared.

"How did you get your leg back?" she asked.

"The Sleeping Death Curse not only sends the unicorns into a deathly state of slumber, it also suppresses their powers, so their Magical Barrier has gone. I no longer need to be under the conjuring spell, as the Holy Isle is now defenceless," Mogdred shrieked at the top of her lungs. "I need you two to remain here and guard the unicorns," she said to Ugg, when she'd finally stopped cackling. "Move the bodies away from the cave entrance, and do not let anyone near them." She handed him the new jar holding Blade. "And take extra care with this, we may need him again."

She scowled at the pair of them threateningly, letting them know that they'd better not lose Blade again.

Mogdred then turned to Serena.

"I want *you* with me," she said. Suddenly blasting Serena in the stomach with a thunderbolt, she snapped her fingers and vanished in a cloud of ash.

"How did she do that?" Ogg asked, with a blank expression on his face. "Didn't we have to do the whole conjuring thing because she can't just enter, or leave, the Holy Isle?"

"That was before she cursed the unicorns," Ugg answered. "Without their Magical Barrier protecting the Holy Isle, Mogdred and her army of Night Witches can come and go as they please."

"But why would she want to come to the Holy Isle?" Ogg persisted.

Ugg beamed back at him with a vicious grin.

"To take the Eagalach Cup!"

Chapter 14

Cornflower Pixies

Gracie was practising catching the ball from behind when she saw a shimmer of green light radiate across the sky.

" Look – that's strange," she said to Snoddy, who was putting in extra training before the Eagalach Cup Final. "I've never seen the sky turn green at night before."

"Me neither," replied Snoddy. "But there is an old nursery rhyme about it:

Green sky in the day –
the unicorns are out to play.
Green sky in the night –
you're in for a big scary fright!"

They both began laughing at the silly rhyme, then resumed their tough training schedule.

The training grounds were on the far side of the village from the stadium. It was a much less impressive venue than the stadium itself, with only a few benches scattered around the edges of the grass pitch.

The pitch itself, however, was an exact replica of the

pitch at the stadium, right down to the odd rogue clump of grass sticking out of the otherwise perfectly mowed lawn.

Gracie decided to call it a night after four hours of gruelling training. She walked over the bench where she had left her rucksack and sat down to untie her laces.

As she lifted her foot onto the bench she could hear someone sniggering behind her,

"Nice shoes," said the intruder.

Gracie whipped round to see which cheeky little pixie had sneaked into the training grounds.

Instead of a naughty little fan standing in front of her, she was greeted by eleven pixies, all wearing bright blue lederhosen.

"Oh great," she thought. "The Cornflower Pixies have arrived a day early."

The Cornflower Pixies were the Eagalach Cup champions, having won the final more than any other pixie clan. Because of their fame they had become quite arrogant and were often rude to their opponents. Today was no exception.

"How cute – they're pink," the ringleader of the group laughed to his team mates.

"No, they're not," shouted Gracie as she continued to untie her yellow trainers.

"It's just with you being a little girlie, we thought maybe yellow had become the new pink in the Pixie Clan," he said.

Thoroughly riled, Gracie jumped to her feet. "I'll show you pink!"

"Now, now, Gracie," Snoddy interjected, putting his hand on Gracie's shoulder. "Obviously the Cornflower Pixies are just a bit nervous about playing against us…

why else would eleven of them round on 'one little girlie'?" The ringleader of the Cornflower Pixies was about the same height and build as Snoddy, but unlike Snoddy with his short beard, the Cornflower Pixie was clean-shaven with a chisel jaw and teeth so white they dazzled when he smiled. This was in fact his special talent on the playing field. He would smile at his opponents to dazzle them, then steal the ball. This trait had earned him the nickname 'Dazzler'.

"We're not nervous about playing a bunch of pixies running around in skirts," Dazzler snapped back at Snoddy. His bouffant hair was starting to frizz at the ends from the steam now bellowing out of his ears.

"That's rich coming from a guy wearing a pair of hot pants!" Snoddy retorted.

Just at that moment Gracie dropped her rucksack. It landed right on top of Snoddy's foot. He bent down to pick it up, and as he did so, Dazzler's punch swung straight over his head, lamping his team mate Crusher, square on the jaw.

There was a loud crunch as Dazzler's hand bounced off Crusher's jawbone.

"Ouch!" Dazzler screamed out in agony.

Crusher looked at him without so much as flinching.

"I'll get you for that," Dazzler growled at Snoddy, clenching his crumpled hand.

"I'm glad you think so," Snoddy replied. He picked up Gracie's rucksack and hitched it over his shoulder, then turned to walk out of the training grounds with Gracie.

"I'm not finished with you," Dazzler shouted after him.

"But I'm finished with you," Snoddy called back.

"For now!" he whispered to Gracie with a wink. "Oh, and thanks for seeing that sneaky punch coming, Gracie."

"Anytime," she smiled back.

After Snoddy and Gracie had left the training ground, the Cornflower Pixies got into a huddle to discuss their strategy for the game.

The Cornflower Pixie team consisted of the captain, Dazzler who was also a runner along with four other runners, plus Crusher, the keeper, five clinchers and two substitutes. The substitutes hadn't arrived yet, as they were still in the changing rooms having their hair sprayed up.

Dazzler instructed his team on their positions.

"You three will play up front," he said to the three smallest runners. "And you'll play at the back with me" he told the tallest runner.

He positioned the five clinchers along the side-lines. The Clinchers all had really short hair to make them more aerodynamic, and huge hands for catching the ball.

For the practice game, they had brought a Scurry Ball and eleven eager fans to play against.

Dazzler and Klein, the shortest of the clinchers, carried the Ball Box to the centre of the pitch.

"Take your positions," Dazzler shouted, then he threw open the box.

Inside it stood a black and white patched ball with two big round eyes and two legs.

The ball seemed to be a little dazed when it stepped out of the box. As its eyes came into focus, it scanned the pitch, looking for the most direct route into one of the nets.

One of the runners tiptoed up behind it, but the ball heard the grass rustling and took flight in the direction of the net currently being defended by Crusher.

"Get it," Dazzler shouted across the pitch to the runners who were up front.

The ball caught a glimpse of his dazzling white teeth out of the corner of its eye and the glare gave it such a shock that it started sprinting even faster towards the goal.

Crusher leaned forward to grab the ball with his arms, but he was too slow and it ran straight through his legs and into the back of the net.

"Why didn't you crush it?" Dazzler hollered into Crusher's face.

"I didn't want to hurt the little guy," Crusher replied in a docile tone.

"You're supposed to stop it getting past you," Dazzler yelled. "You're called Crusher for a reason… it's because you are supposed to crush things."

"I crush things – not people," Crusher replied defensively.

"It's a ball, NOT a person!" Dazzler shrieked, exasperated by Crusher's stupidity. "They don't feel anything – they're specially trained to run towards the net! Oh, never mind" he continued, unable to keep the frustration out of his voice. "You just better hope Mr Frankenhouzen doesn't find out about this."

"Find out about what?" a man's voice echoed from the other side of the pitch.

Mr Frankenhouzen did not look like the other Cornflower Pixies. He was dressed in a smart black suit with a black shirt, orange cravat and a matching handkerchief, which had been carefully placed in the breast pocket of the jacket.

"Erm, nothing to be concerned about," Dazzler replied nervously.

"Oh, so the fact that my keeper is too soft to crush a ball is nothing to be concerned about," Mr Frankenhouzen roared.

"That's not what I meant," replied Dazzler sheepishly. "I'm sure we can convince Crusher that the balls can't feel anything is what I meant."

"And why would we need to do that, when he is no longer on the team?" replied Mr Frankenhouzen with an evil glint in his eye.

"But he's the only keeper we have," pleaded Dazzler.

"Not anymore," Mr Frankenhouzen said confidently, as he ushered a huge figure of a pixie onto the pitch. "Meet Slayer."

Dazzler gulped. The ground trembled with Slayer's every step. Slayer was a full head taller than Dazzler and twice as wide. Three of his front teeth were missing and he was sporting a black eye.

"Who's going to tell Crusher? He'll be devastated!" asked Dazzler.

"Well, you're the captain," said Mr Frankenhouzen, looking down his nose at him. "I believe that's your job… unless I need to find a replacement for you too?"

"No, no, it's fine. I'll tell him." The glint had most definitely gone from Dazzler's smile as he lugged himself across the pitch towards his team mates and his former keeper.

Chapter 15

The Wicked Wand

Hour after hour, Thumble Tumble and McCools searched to find a way out of the Box Aplenty. They climbed up the shelves to the top of the box and tried to push the lid open, but it was sealed tight from the outside.

They examined behind the shelves, looking for the invisible door McCools had once misplaced inside the magic box, but the closest thing they found to a door was a rusty old door knob.

"I told you those Rascal Goblins are dangerous," said McCools as he clambered back down to the floor.

"Well there's no point in gloating about it now," sighed Thumble Tumble. "Not while we're still stuck inside this oversized storage crate."

"Are you sure you can't conjure just a little spell?" McCools asked hopefully.

"I've told you before… I can't do magic without a wand!"

Thumble Tumble folded her arms crossly.

The pair sat on the floor staring at the witch's broom they had recovered from behind the scarves.

"Wait a minute," said McCools, thinking aloud. "Did you say 'a wand'?"

"Yes," replied, Thumble Tumble. "I'm pretty sure any wand would work."

"Then we might just be in luck," McCools smiled. "I thought wands would only work for their owner."

"That's just a rumour made up by wizards to try to stop people from stealing their wands," explained Thumble Tumble. "The only hitch is when a good witch tries to use an evil wand, or vice versa."

"Oh, so you can't use a Night Witch's wand then?" said McCools, deflated.

"I can use it," she replied. "It's just that sometimes the spells come out a bit wonky. You see, the evil wand will jinx the spell to kill the good witch trying to use it."

"That's a shame," McCools said despondently.

"Why?" asked Thumble Tumble.

"Because I'm sure I have an old Night Witch's wand in here somewhere."

"Then let's find it!" she cried out, jumping to her feet.

"But what about the jinxing spells?" he said anxiously.

"I'd rather take my chances with a Night Witch's wand rather than waiting here hoping the Rascal Goblin returns to set us free – wouldn't you?" Thumble Tumble said, putting out her hand to help McCools onto his three legs. "So, where is this Night Witch's wand?" she asked, clapping her hands.

"That's another possible slight obstacle," said McCools, frowning. "I can't quite remember where I put it."

"Oh, great," sighed Thumble Tumble. "It will take us weeks to search all of these shelves."

"I'm sure it was also near my scarves... I like to keep all of my witch memorabilia together," McCools muttered, deep in concentration.

Thumble Tumble quickly climbed back up to the shelf where McCools' scarves were bundled. She pulled out every single scarf, including a bright yellow woolly one that had a matching hat.

She picked up the hat and waved it down at McCools. "I didn't have you pegged as a hat guy," she laughed.

"It was a gift," McCools replied curtly, a pink glow appearing on his cheeks. "Any sign of the wand?" he asked, quickly changing the subject.

"Not yet... A gift you say?" she continued, noticing McCools was blushing.

"Let's focus on the wand rather than my hat," he said.

"OK, well there's nothing here but a bunch of pens," Thumble Tumble shouted down. "Where did you get all these pens anyway?"

"I just picked them up on my travels. Whenever anyone hands me a pen to sign something I like to hold on to it," he said casually.

"So you just pinch them," she giggled.

"I do nothing of the sort," replied McCools in an offended tone. "I treat them as gifts."

"Just like your yellow hat?" she quipped back.

McCools sat down on the floor with his arms folded and ignored her.

"I'm sorry, McCools," Thumble Tumble called down, realising she'd upset him.

In an attempt to make amends, she decided to

compliment him on his wonderful collection of things.

"I really like your pen collection," she said, but McCools just kept looking at the floor. "Especially the wooden pen," she continued. "I've never seen one of those before."

"Wooden pen?" McCools said, breaking his silence. "I don't have a wooden pen."

"Well there's definitely one up here," Thumble Tumble said, reaching for it. But as soon as her fingertips got near the pen, it started to roll away. She stretched her arm a bit more, and as she did, the pen rolled a bit further.

Thumble Tumble picked up a feather quill and used it to try to flick the wooden pen towards her. But the wooden pen started quivering, as though it was being tickled. Thumble Tumble saw her chance.

"Got it!" she shouted triumphantly, just as the pen slipped through her fingers and rolled straight back to the rear of the shelf.

Thumble Tumble picked the quill up again, and gently rubbed the feather against the wooden pen. When the wooden pen started to wriggle, she shot both hands forward and grabbed it tightly between them. As soon as she touched the pen, it began rising into the air, then flew off the shelf, leaving Thumble Tumble once again dangling in mid-air. The pen tried to shake itself free from her grip, but she didn't let go. She had felt this type of wood before… it was the feeling she had when holding a wand.

"I've found the wand," she called out.

"Then bring it down," said McCools.

"I'm trying to," she said, now being given a frantic shaking by the wand. "Descendio!" she shouted.

The wand instantly charged towards the ground, taking Thumble Tumble with it. Just before it crashed on the floor, she let go.

Thumble Tumble slowly floated for a few inches before gently landing beside the wand.

"This one's feisty," said McCools, standing on the wand with one foot. "It just tried to splat you!"

"If it thinks it can harm me by jinxing the spell – then it will!" said Thumble Tumble. She looked back up at one of the shelves. "I have an idea," she whispered into McCools' ear.

She dashed off to the back of the box and reappeared a few moments later holding the old door knob they had discarded earlier. It was a round brass knob covered in scratches and dents. Thumble Tumble leaned down and took the wand from under McCools' foot. She pointed it at the door handle. "Repairio!" she said. A thin drizzle of light left the tip of the wand and wrapped itself around the door-knob. The knob spun in the air and when it stopped it was as good as new, gleaming and dent free.

Thumble Tumble popped the wand back under

McCools' foot and ran over to a gap between the shelves. She placed the door-knob onto the wall and as she did the outline of a door appeared around it.

"Hurry up," she said anxiously. "We only have a few moments."

McCools took the wand from under his foot, picked up the broom and dashed over towards the newly formed doorway.

Thumble Tumble turned the brass knob and the door swung open. They quickly stepped back through into McCools' Broom Cupboard before it slammed shut. A few seconds later, and the door was gone.

"It was a universal door knob," explained Thumble Tumble, smiling over at a rather confused looking McCools. "It fits any door, even an invisible one. So, when I repaired it, it found your mislaid invisible door. The wand didn't think repairing an old door-knob was of any use to us, which is why it didn't jinx the spell. Now all we need to do is get this broom working," she added, pointing at the rickety old broom in his hand.

"And for that we'll need some broom powder," said McCools.

"How will we get a hold of broom powder all the way up here?" asked Thumble Tumble.

"We'll borrow some from my neighbour."

"I didn't know you had any neighbours."

McCools cast her a roguish grin. "There's a lot you don't know about me, Thumble Tumble!"

Chapter 16

Fire Starter

Ugg and Ogg decided to set up camp right outside the unicorn cave, even though they had been given strict instructions to move the unicorns' bodies away from the entrance.

"They weigh a ton," groaned Ugg, as he tried to pick one of them up onto his shoulders. The weight of the paralysed unicorn was way too much for him. His legs gave way, sending him and the unicorn crashing to the ground. "I don't see why we need to move them," he grumbled as he got back onto his feet. "It's not like they're going anywhere." He kicked, the defenceless unicorn with his stump.

"But won't Mogdred be mad at us if we leave them here?" quavered Ogg, still traumatised after being turned into a frog.

"She won't know," Ugg replied assertively. "And what Mogdred doesn't know, can't make her mad." Ugg took the jar with Blade inside and placed it on the sand beside the unicorns. He then got a large stone and sat it on top of the lid. "That'll stop you pulling off another escapade." He turned to Ogg. "Why don't you go find us something to eat and I'll start a fire?"

Ogg obediently headed off to forage for food whilst Ugg combed the beach looking for driftwood. When he had gathered enough wood for a fire he scanned the surface of the water. "Perfect!" he cried, lunging forward to seize a tiny firefly that was hovering just above the wash.

He shook the firefly until it turned red, then pressed its body against the pile of wood until a small flame appeared. He quickly pulled his hand back from the fire, as being made of wood and bark himself, he was highly flammable.

He then popped the little firefly in his mouth. "Yummy," he murmured as he chomped.

The firefly slid down his throat and into his stomach, giving him a lovely warm sensation inside. He could feel beads of sweat rolling down his forehead as he smacked his lips, and his tummy began to feel very hot.

He looked down to rub it…

"*Yikes!*" he screamed. "*I'm on fire!*" The red-hot firefly had set his insides ablaze and flames were shooting out of his stomach. Ugg ran to the water's edge and threw himself in face-first. A loud hissing sound rose-up from the water as the flames died off.

When he was fully 'out', he dragged himself from the water and set about repairing his stomach by stuffing it with twigs and leaves.

Ogg wasn't having much luck either. He had looked under every tree trunk, stone and leaf he came across and hadn't found so much as a slug. Or at least that's what he decided he was going to tell Ugg as he gorged himself on his hoard of juicy slugs. When he returned to camp he found Ugg lying asleep beside the fire with a huge bandage wrapped around his waist.

He checked that the unicorns were still completely immobilised, and saw that Blade was snoozing peacefully in his glass prison.

He picked up the stone off the lid and rattled it against the side of the jar. Blade woke up with a start. Ogg burst out laughing and placed the stone back on top of the lid.

"Wakey, wakey!" he waved in at Blade.

A huge drop of saliva drooled out of his mouth, fell onto the side of the jar and slowly tricked down. Ogg could feel a grumbling sensation in his stomach.

"What Mogdred doesn't know won't make her mad." He started humming to himself as he once again removed the stone from the lid of the jar and looked around furtively before slowly unscrewing the lid. He extended his branchy fingers into the jar and grabbed Blade by his wings.

"Mogdred won't be happy," Blade yelled up at the salivating monster now lowering him into its mouth.

Ogg closed his eyes and let go of Blade's wings, ready to savour his mini feast. But instead of feeling a delicious Flower Nymph on his tongue, all he felt was a whack on the side of his head, from the rock Ugg had just thrown at him.

Blade fell straight onto Ugg's open palm and was promptly shoved back inside the jar.

"We can always move the unicorns if Mogdred returns," Ugg lectured. "But we can't undigest the Flower

Nymph if you eat him! I take it you didn't find any food?"

"No, I didn't find any juicy big slugs," lied Ogg, still dazed.

"Oh, well never mind. Let's try to get some sleep. That should help take our minds off hunger," said Ugg.

The Tree Trolls lay down beside the fire and started snoring like a couple of elephants who'd caught the cold.

Meanwhile, Serena had woken up inside Mogdred's dungeon with a dreadful pain in her stomach, mostly from having been struck by a lightning bolt. The dungeon was dimly lit by a few candles dotted around the walls.

She could hear raised voices coming from the far corner of the chamber, but it was so dark she couldn't see who was doing all the shouting.

She edged her way along the wall, desperately looking for any sign of her sister, Alfy, but sadly she seemed to have been moved... again.

As she drew near to it, she could make out the image of a large rectangular table with seven figures seated around it. Mogdred was sitting at the head of the table, with her daughters Gretch and Sloth perched on either side of her.

Opposite Mogdred sat Tabathay, the supreme Troll Witch. She had a long thin body and an oversized head.

"The Holy Isle has the protection of the unicorns," she was hissing across the table at Mogdred. "My Troll Witches will disintegrate as soon as they touch it."

"The unicorns have been taken care of," Mogdred assured her. "We can take the Holy Isle whenever we wish."

"And how do we know this isn't just one of your traps? For all we know the magical barrier is still there and it will destroy us, leaving you free to take over our territories,"

Tabathay retorted, banging her fists down on the table.

"You may as well show yourself," Mogdred suddenly addressed Serena. "We know you're listening."

Serena stepped out of the shadows.

"Tell them about the unicorns," Mogdred growled.

"It's true," said Serena. "The unicorns are trapped. The Holy Isle is defenceless."

"See!" Gretch and Sloth hissed in unison, glaring at Tabathay.

"How did you manage to capture the unicorns?" asked one of the other witches at the table. "They can smell the foul breath of a Night Witch for miles."

"Not if the Night Witch's breath is masked by the scent of a rosebud," Mogdred cackled.

"A rosebud can't hide your odour," the witch spat back.

Mogdred soared above the table, her long black finger pointing straight at the witch's heart.

"Mind your manners," she roared. "It wasn't any old rosebud. It was the scent of a Rose Nymph."

"Oh, I do apologise," the witch grovelled.

"And the unicorns are secure?" Tabathay interjected in a much less hostile tone, now reminded of Mogdred's deathly temper, and even more deadly index finger.

"They are under the curse of the Sleeping Death, being held captive by two of my guards," Mogdred told her.

"That's all very well," Tabathay continued. "But how do we know you won't just take the Eagalach Cup for yourself, and use it to take over the dark realm?"

Mogdred's face contorted into an even uglier expression than normal as she rose high into the air, spreading her hands out above the table.

"Do you think I need a stupid cup to give me the power

of destruction?" her voice echoed through the dungeon. "I can send out one hundred Thunder Bolts in the blink of an eye. You can have the cup," she continued, pointing towards Tabathay. "All I want is the female child who plays Eagalach. Bring me the child and the cup is yours. Now go… round up your armies and join me in the skies above the Holy Isle tomorrow night."

She waved her hand above the table and the four witches who had been sitting opposite her disappeared.

"Why do you want the girl?" Gretch quizzed her mother.

"I will answer that when we no longer have prying ears in our dungeon," Mogdred replied, turning a demonic stare on Serena. "And you know where you have to be tomorrow night if you ever want to see Alfy again," she said in a threatening tone, before sending another lightning bolt straight into Serena's stomach.

Chapter 17

Cheating Tactics

After waiting patiently all day, the time had finally come for Gracie to join her team mates in the changing rooms. The players were decked out in pristine new strips – a black and purple check kilt and a white top with the words 'Thistle Pixie Clan' emblazoned across the front in dark purple, with their team number printed on the back.

Scoutt's dark purple armband identified him as captain and Rocky was wearing his keeper's protective helmet (this was to allow him to header the ball away without it kicking him on his head!).

LB wasn't on the team, but he'd come down to the changing rooms to wish his friends luck. Scoutt was just about to start his pep-talk when LB walked in.

"Will I come back later?" he asked, hoping to escape one of Scoutt's lengthy talks.

"Don't be silly," answered Snoddy patting LB on the back as he walked him into the changing rooms. "You take a comfy seat – you'll need it for this speech."

With a cheesy grin, he plonked LB down on the bench beside Gracie.

Gracie budged over to give him some room and continued lacing her oversized gloves. Gracie was a Clincher, but because she didn't have particularly big hands she wore special gloves that were ten times bigger than her actual hand size.

Her hair had been squeezed into a beanie cap to help with aerodynamics and she was wearing her favourite yellow trainers.

Next to Gracie were the other four clinchers – Eck, Finn, Rhu and Titch.

Eck was the oldest player on the team. He had been playing Eagalach since he was just four years old and was renowned as one of the world's best clinchers. He had red hair that had been shaved to his scalp, and a neatly trimmed beard.

Finn – the youngest player on the team (with the exception of Gracie) – was so fast and agile, he was being branded the next 'Posh Boy'. His Mohican hairstyle had been dyed purple for the game, and the female supporters loved him.

Rhu was the same height as Gracie, with short, spiky, saffron-coloured hair and eyes to match. He wore bright yellow gloves with a love-heart pattern on the palms. The idea was that if the ball spotted him, they'd see the love-heart pattern and so wouldn't run away. The plan hadn't actually worked in the past, but Rhu really liked the gloves.

Next to Rhu was Titch, the smallest player on the team. Titch was so small his legs dangled off the edge of the bench. He sat through the entire pep-talk staring at the ceiling, daydreaming about the Thistle Pixies winning the Eagalach Cup.

After twenty-two minutes of non-stop chat, Scoutt finally uttered the words the whole team had been waiting for. "Now let me pass over to Fergus for a few words."

Everyone immediately gave the manager one hundred per cent concentration. Even Titch took a break from his daydream.

Fergus was a legend in the game of Eagalach.

He rose off the bench and took a wad of paper out of his pocket. He unfolded his notes and began to read: "To win the Eagalach Cup you need courage, determination and stamina". He looked around the room at the players all eagerly staring towards him, then crushed the paper in his hand. "You don't need this speech," he said defiantly. "I just need to glance around this room and I can see you have what it takes to win the cup – so just go out there and do it!"

The changing room erupted into a ruckus of cheering and when the roar finally died down the players made their way onto the pitch.

It was traditional for each team to sing their clan anthem before the game. First up were the Cornflower Pixies. Dazzler stood with five players on either side of him. They all had immaculately preened hair and were wearing their customised, glitter encrusted, bright blue lederhosen strips – all except Slayer, whose strip was a bit too tight, and instead of glitter, he'd had a skull and crossbones stitched onto the bib of his lederhosen.

The Cornflower Pixie orchestra on the side-lines struck up and the team began to bellow out the Cornflower anthem.

The stadium was packed to the gunnells with supporters from both clans, sitting together to represent the harmony of the game. As soon as the orchestra began playing, all of the Cornflower Pixies stood up waving their clan's flags above their heads.

The Cornflower players held hands and lifted their arms in the air to reveal ten beautiful female pixies, wearing stunning blue gowns that flowed along the ground as they walked under the players' arching arms.

The female choir began to sing the Cornflower anthem, then an array of dancers and acrobats appeared on the pitch, performing all manner of stunts.

When the choir finished, each of the ladies held up a canister from which mini rockets launched into the sky, filling it with blue sparkles.

The Cornflower supporters began stamping their feet, clapping and chanting: "Corn! Corn! Corn!"

Dazzler smiled over at Scoutt. "We like to start as we mean to finish," he said, shaking his blue bouffant hair in the air. "Winners!"

Scoutt looked straight through him, without so much as a twitch. When the fireworks were finally over, a sole Thistle Pixie walked out to the centre of the pitch holding a set of bagpipes. He was in traditional dress, kilt and gillie shirt. He took a deep breath and began to play the Thistle Pixie anthem.

After a few moments, the lone musician was joined by Titch. The tiny Clincher left his team formation and walked over to stand beside the piper. He paused for a second, then he began to sing the Thistle Pixie anthem.

His angelic voice, soft and sweet, had an eerie hypnotic effect and the entire stadium began swaying from side to

side in time with him. By the time he finished, there wasn't a dry eye in the place. Even the Cornflower supporters were crying. The two musicians took a bow, at which point the Thistle Pixie supporters broke into song: 'Come on the Thistles'.

Titch returned to his team mates, who were now being briefed by the referee.

"I want a good, clean game," the ref said, wagging his index finger as he addressed the Thistle Pixie players, his back turned to the Cornflower team.

There were murmurs of laughter behind him as the Cornflower players giggled at Dazzler impersonating the referee behind his back.

"I could book you for that," the referee said, without even turning around.

Dazzler immediately stood back in line with the rest of his team mates.

When he had finished with the Thistle Pixies, the referee repeated the same warning, word for word, to the Cornflower team.

The referee was wearing his golden whistle around his

neck and his chest was so inflated with pride, it looked as if he breathed too hard, he might burst. His grey hair was combed into a smart side-shed and his beard had been neatly trimmed up to his waist in preparation for the big game.

When the noise in the stadium settled down, he turned to the linesmen. "Bring out the ball!" he hollered with his chin held high.

Two linesmen appeared from the tunnel carrying a small black box with holes on top, which they deposited on the grass in the centre of the pitch.

"Are you ready?" he asked the two captains now standing face to face on the pitch. Both Scoutt and Dazzler nodded. The referee blew his whistle, simultaneously throwing open the lid of the box.

The Bolt Ball came hurtling out, aiming directly for the Thistle Pixie goal.

"Get after it, Blurr!" shouted Scoutt.

Blurr was one of the Thistle Pixie runners. He could run so fast, that if you watched him, all you'd get was a blurred image of him running past you.

Blurr shot after the ball as fast as he could, but the ball wasn't for being caught and it managed to keep a full three feet in front of him as it pelted towards the back of the Thistle Pixie net.

Rocky was standing ready to catch the ball, legs apart and arms out to the side in order to fill as much of the goal as possible.

The Bolt Ball was travelling so fast, Rocky couldn't keep his eyes on it. Suddenly it was at his feet and was about to run through the gap between his legs when Scoutt came sprinting in from the side and kicked it off course.

Scoutt raced after the ball, trying to get it to run towards the Cornflower goal, but instead it ran right off the pitch. Gracie was already standing in position, and the ball ran straight into her hands.

The ball tugged to get free but Gracie held on fast, then threw it towards Rocky who headed it three quarters of the way down the pitch where it hit the ground like a tiny tornado, whizzing between the Cornflower players on its way towards their goal.

Blurr chased after the ball, and this time he was catching up. He was two inches away when he slammed into the ground, his jaw swollen from the force of Slayer's fist.

The referee blew his golden whistle and everyone stood still – even the Bolt Ball. During 'Time Out' the ball would take a rest along with the players.

"What happened here?" blasted the referee.

"He punched me," Blurr howled, still lying on the ground nursing his broken jaw.

"I did not," insisted Slayer. "He ran straight into my fist as I was trying to stop the ball. Didn't he Dazzler?"

"Yes, that's right, ref." Dazzler almost choked on the words. He had never cheated at a game of Eagalach in his life before and it left a bad feeling in his stomach doing it now.

He had seen Slayer's fist hit off Blurr's jaw. But he hadn't been trying to get the ball. Dazzler had already kicked it clear. Slayer had deliberately punched Blurr to injure him!

Dazzler looked over at the side-lines where Mr Frankenhouzen was standing with his index finger pressed against his lips and a wicked glare in his eye, indicating to

Dazzler that he'd better keep quiet.

"I'm afraid it's two against one, Blurr," said the referee, shaking his head. "I'll have to go with Slayer's version of events. Are you OK to play on?"

"Yes, I'll just get an ice-pack," Blurr mumbled back, barely able to open his mouth from the swelling.

Everyone resumed their positions and the referee blew his whistle to continue with the game.

The next thirty minutes passed with no goals, but there were several more mysterious injuries to the Thistle Pixies inflicted by Slayer – all witnessed by Dazzler.

Two runners had to be taken off with a crushed foot, after Slayer had 'accidentally' stood on them whilst trying to kick the ball. And Titch had his nose broken when Slayer bent down, apparently to header the ball, but inadvertently head-butted Titch instead.

The referee blew his whistle for a full three seconds to announce half time and both teams wearily headed off the pitch towards their respective changing rooms.

Chapter 18

The Clairvoyant

McCools popped his tartan scarf around his neck and handed Thumble Tumble her cloak, before they headed out into the cold evening air.

"So, who is this neighbour of yours?" asked Thumble Tumble, intrigued by McCools' secret neighbour.

"She's a witch" replied McCools. "A retired Night Witch, to be precise."

"A Night Witch?" gasped Thumble Tumble.

"Retired!" McCools said reassuringly.

"I didn't know Night Witches retired."

"Neither did I, until I met Elezdra," explained McCools. "She came here around about the time Mogdred decided she wanted to take over the coven. Elezdra was one of the few Night Witches who stood up to Mogdred, and for her disobedience she was stripped of her wand and banished. Mogdred cast her out on a broom at midday. Elezdra was blinded by the scorching sunlight and she crashed into the cliff just a few hundred yards from here. I was taking my usual Tuesday ramble along the cliff. She was all but dead when I found her body in the snow. I managed to carry her to my house and spent several weeks nursing her back to health. Unfortunately, the damage to her eyes was irreversible, even for someone with my extensive knowledge of anatomy. And so, she remains blind to this day."

"Did she turn good after all that?" asked Thumble Tumble.

"No, no," laughed McCools. "She's still a Night Witch, so evil runs in her veins. But, she owes me her life, and Mogdred, her death! Elezdra made a vow on the day she woke from her frozen sleep. She vowed to repay me for saving her life, and, to do everything in her power to bring down Mogdred." He fumbled around in the snow. "

It's around here somewhere." "What is?"

"Her door." He continued as he kicked and prodded the snow.

"Ah, here it is."

A little stone cottage with a thatched roof seemed to have appeared out of nowhere. She bounded over with her fist clenched ready to knock on the wooden door.

"Stop right there," shouted McCools. "Haven't you learned it's impolite to knock on an enchanted door?" He knelt in the snow and whispered into the keyhole: "Two we be, and Elezdra we wish to see."

The door spoke back as it swung open:

"In here Elezdra you will find,

but hurry up, before I change my mind!"

The door then began to close.

"Quick as you can," McCools said to Thumble Tumble.

The cottage was in complete darkness, but a few

seconds after they entered, dozens of candles self-combusted.

The cottage seemed to consist of just one room. The two windows on the back wall had wooden slats nailed over them. In one corner, there was a cauldron bubbling on top of a fire and in the other stood a crystal ball, with images of the outside of the cottage flashing up inside it.

There was a bed perched against the wall under the windows with a rocking chair beside it. The person in the bed was completely covered by a huge dark blanket. Sitting in the chair, there was a young witch rocking back and forth, watching over whoever was in the bed.

"Elezdra wants you to come closer," said the young witch. McCools stepped forward with Thumble Tumble approaching more cautiously, from behind him.

"Elezdra must feel your hand," the young witch continued in a haunting voice.

McCools put out his hand. The young witch took hold of his hand and slowly rubbed it.

"Oh, it's you McCools," the young witch said, shaking her head. Within a split second the young witch's face had morphed into the face of an old hag with dark grey skin sagging off her bones. Both her eyes were covered with black eye patches that looked as though they'd been stitched onto her face.

"And, we won't be needing this," she said, as she pulled the blanket off the bed to reveal a massive bear trap, prized open ready to chomp off someone's limb.

"You can never be too careful," she cackled.

"This is…" McCools gestured towards Thumble Tumble.

"I know who she is," Elezdra snapped, cutting him off.

"She is the one," she intoned hauntingly, and started probing Thumble Tumble's face with her fingers.

"There's no need to be so dramatic," said McCools. "I know she is the new Protector, but there have been many others before her."

The Protector is a witch with very special powers. Their role is to defend the Witch's Coven against its enemies, and to allow them to do this they are bestowed with powers from every species of witch on earth. Although she didn't know it yet, Thumble Tumble was an extremely powerful witch.

"She's more important than you know," said Elezdra. "She is the one who will help me fulfil my vow."

"The vow to bring down Mogdred?" Thumble Tumble interjected, waving Elezdra's hands away from her face.

"Perhaps," Elezdra replied with a loud cackle. She turned to the wall. "Now, what do you need from me?"

McCools tapped her on the back. "I'm here," he said.

"I know that," Elezdra said, spinning round. "I was speaking to the girl."

Thumble Tumble was standing right beside McCools, but chose not to say anything as she didn't want to embarrass Elezdra.

"Thank you for your discretion," Elezdra said, nodding directly at Thumble Tumble.

"We need some broom powder to get this thing flying again," McCools said, holding out the broom so that Elezdra could feel it.

"Mmm, solid oak," she murmured. "You'll need a fair bit of broom powder to get this thing off the ground. Let me see what I have in my cauldron."

She felt her way along the wall towards the crystal ball, then exclaimed, "Oops, wrong corner!" As she turned to walk to the opposite corner, her hand brushed against the crystal ball. Elezdra froze on the spot. The images of the outside of the cottage floating through the crystal ball were replaced by a thick green smoke, and the patches covering Elezdra's eyes had also changed. They now had green flames shooting out of them.

"I see grave danger," she said, speaking in a harrowing tone. "Beware of the trees – they are not what they seem."

The flames in her eyes then extinguished as quickly as they'd come and her crystal returned to monitoring the outside of the cottage.

"Sorry about that," said Elezdra, and continued feeling

her way towards the cauldron.

"What just happened?" Thumble Tumble whispered to McCools.

"Elezdra is a clairvoyant," replied McCools. "She can see into the future."

"Oh, just like Gracie with her bracelet?" Thumble Tumble asked.

"Similar," said McCools. "The difference is, Gracie can look into the future whenever she wants with the power of the bracelet. Elezdra only sees what the crystal chooses to show her. And, it's usually when something terrible is about to happen!"

"Oh," gulped Thumble Tumble.

"Don't worry," smiled McCools. "Her predictions aren't always accurate."

Elezdra reached the cauldron, and began stirring the contents with a wooden spoon in an anti-clockwise direction.

After a few minutes she put down the spoon and rummaged inside her cloak. She produced a small cloth bag.

"Here you go," she said to McCools, handing him the bag. "This is all the broom powder I have."

"Thank you," he replied, staring curiously at the cauldron. "What's in the cauldron?"

"This is the gravy for my dinner," Elezdra replied, with a big grin that exposed her black pointy teeth.

A shiver ran down McCools back.

Elezdra may have retired, but she was still a Night Witch! And they are partial to children, with a nice dollop of gravy!

"Come on Thumble Tumble," McCools said anxiously.

"It's time for us to go."

"Oh, what a shame you can't stay for dinner," Elezdra said, inching her way along the wall towards them.

"Maybe next time," McCools called over his shoulder as he pushed Thumble Tumble out the front door and slammed it shut behind them.

Chapter 19

Half Time

Fergus greeted each of his players with a pat on the back as they entered the changing room.

The team were absolutely exhausted as they slumped onto the benches.

Four Thistle Pixies dressed in white gowns scurried around the room examining the players. One was carrying a little clip-board and calling out instructions to the other three.

"Water," he said, pointing at Snoddy.

"Ice-pack," he gestured towards Finn.

"Water and ice-pack," he said, as they passed Rhu.

The team were down to eight players thanks to Slayer's 'accidents'. Not only that, but their two substitutes had also mysteriously disappeared from the side-lines.

When everyone was seated, and had been seen by the pixie medics, Fergus once again took centre stage.

"Well done guys," he said. "You're playing as well as I could hope, but I need to ask you for more. We all know the other side are up to no good. They've taken out three of our team and done goodness knows what with our substitutes. We need to be a step ahead of them. Gracie, can you focus in on Slayer and see which player he plans to 'accidentally' bump into next?"

"Sure can, boss," replied Gracie.

"As soon as you know, I want you to shout out their name three times." Fergus glanced around at his team. "If you hear your name called out three times, I want you to run as fast as you can *away* from Slayer. He is such a stupid oaf, that he'll leave the goal to chase after his prey. I need the rest of you to get the ball to Rocky the minute Slayer leaves his position – got it?"

Everyone nodded back, even the medics.

Fergus then addressed Rocky. "You need to header that ball all the way up the pitch and into his goal."

Rocky gulped. "I'll do my best, skipper."

"I know you will," said Fergus.

He sat back down as the pixie medics carried out one last check over the players.

Mr Frankenhouzen was also waiting to greet his team as they entered their changing room. As each player walked through the door, he kicked them from behind, pushing them towards the benches.

Every player was subjected to this vile reception, with the exception of Slayer, who was greeted with a huge bucket of toad's liver.

The players collapsed onto the benches having been run ragged for forty-five minutes.

"What on earth do you call that?" Mr Frankenhouzen sneered. "I've seen more effort from a Tweezel Berry hanging from a bush! If it wasn't for Slayer you'd have been destroyed out there," he continued, pointing in the direction of the pitch.

"To be fair, they are playing a pretty good game," Dazzler piped up, now completely fed up with Mr Frankenhouzen's bullying tactics, not to mention his cheating.

"Oh, really!" Mr Frankenhouzen roared as he rounded on Dazzler. "Well if they're so-o-o good, maybe you should play for them... now that you're no longer playing for me!" He ripped Dazzler's blue arm-band off and handed it to Slayer. "You're the captain now," he said, sneering towards Dazzler.

"Suits me," Dazzler retorted. "I couldn't stomach another moment of your cheating tactics... I'd rather be thrashed on the pitch, than subject myself to the humiliation of cheating."

The other players watched in dismay as Dazzler picked up his kit bag walked past the two bound and gagged Thistle Pixie substitutes and left the changing room.

"Would anyone else like to join him?" asked Mr Frankenhouzen, glaring around the room.

The players all bowed their heads in silence.

"Very well then," he snapped.

"Let's get down to business. We can't take any chances with these Thistle Pixies, we need to take them out. I want you to lure them one at a time towards Slayer, and he'll do the rest."

Slayer smirked over at him as he spoke, punching his left fist into his right hand.

There was a knock at the door.

"Second half," a voice shouted.

The Cornflower team got to their feet and headed out to join the Thistle Pixies on the pitch.

116

Chapter 20

Crash Landing

As soon as they were outside Elezdra's cottage, McCools poured the whole bag of broom powder onto the oak broom.

The sun had set, so Thumble Tumble was relying on the moonlight reflecting off the snow to allow her to see.

"Levioso!" she said pointing her borrowed wand at the broom. The broom lifted off the ground a couple of feet, then sat hovering in mid-air.

"Well, that's a good start," she said.

"A bit too good," suggested McCools cagily.

Thumble Tumble popped one leg over the broom. "It feels OK too," she said reassuringly.

"Very well," said McCools, as he reluctantly climbed onto the back of the broom and grabbed hold of Thumble Tumble's waist.

"Take me home!" she instructed the broom.

The broom rose high up into the air and started flying in the direction of Thumble Tumble's cottage. The freezing night air cut threw them as they soared high above the clouds.

Thumble Tumble looked down at the scenery below.

"Wait a minute," she said, "we're heading in the wrong direction!"

Thumble Tumble's broom had changed course and was now heading away from her home, in the direction of the Holy Isle. She pulled on the broom's handle trying to get it back on course, but it wouldn't deviate from its new destination.

"It's this wand," she called back to McCools. "It's making us go the long way home!"

"I hope that's all it's doing," McCools replied.

As they flew over the water towards the Holy Isle, the broom started to slow down. Suddenly, they dropped out of the sky like a stone, crashing towards the sea below. Thumble Tumble grabbed the broom, pulling up the nose to try to slow their descent.

"Watch out!" shouted McCools. "If you touch the Magical Barrier you'll disintegrate. Remember that during the Eagalach Cup Final it frazzles all witches – good *or* evil."

Thumble Tumble tugged at the broom with all her might, but her efforts were fruitless.

"You'll need to jump before we get over the Holy Isle... go now!" McCools cried, and he pushed her off the broom.

Thumble Tumble went hurtling over the front of the broom, but her hands were stuck fast to the handle and she whizzed through the air, dangling from it.

McCools tried desperately to prize her fingers loose, but it was no use.

As they shot through the Magical Barrier, Thumble

Tumble clenched her jaws together in preparation of being turned into charcoal.

However, instead of being roasted alive, she crash-landed feet-first onto the beach. As she collided with the ground the broom split in two, instantly releasing her from its magical grip.

Thumble Tumble started patting herself down.

"I didn't disintegrate," she said, delighted.

She looked around to find McCools lying in a heap, still holding onto the back half of the broom. "Are you OK?"

"I think so," replied a dazed McCools.

"I thought I was a goner for sure," sighed Thumble Tumble.

"Me too. There must be something wrong with the magical barrier," McCools said. "Let's find the other half of this broom and get out of here... before they fix it."

The front half of the broom was sticking out of the sand twenty metres along the beach.

"That's a strange pattern," said Thumble Tumble, looking down at the circular pattern in the sand beside where the broomstick had landed. Inside the circle, two triangles had been etched, each pointing in the opposite direction.

"That's not a pattern," said McCools. "That's a symbol. Check the sand to see if there are any more."

Thumble Tumble kicked the top layer of sand with her foot to reveal the outline of a hexagon next to the circle. It too had a drawing inside it. This time it was a crescent moon.

"This doesn't look good," said McCools, kicking the sand to expose a third – a pentagon that had something etched at each of the five tips. They couldn't make out what the patterns had been, as they had been rubbed away by something that looked like a branch.

"This is a conjuring hex," said McCools.

"What does it conjure?" asked Thumble Tumble.

"It's not what… it's who," McCools replied warily. "This spell uses very dark magic and can only be performed by the most powerful, and most evil, of witches."

"But I thought witches couldn't get through the unicorns' Magical Barrier," said Thumble Tumble.

"They can't. But with this spell they do not come through the barrier. They are conjured straight out of the ground!"

"Do you think the symbols have something to do with the magical barrier not working?" Thumble Tumble asked.

"I think they have everything to do with it. We need to get to the unicorn's caves and find out what's going on," McCools said urgently.

"Aren't they hidden in the cliffs?" Thumble Tumble asked anxiously. "How will we ever manage to find them in the dark?"

"I'm pretty sure if we just head towards that smoke we'll be fairly close," McCools said, pointing in the direction of the smoke bellowing up from Ugg and Ogg's fire.

When they arrived at the Tree Trolls' campsite it looked completely deserted. There was nothing other than a few old tree trunks lying on the ground beside the smouldering fire.

"Do you remember Elezdra's prediction?" McCools whispered to Thumble Tumble.

Without answering, she pulled the wand out from her cloak. Pointing it directly towards the tree trunks, she shouted "Revealeo!"

Nothing happened.

Thumble Tumble walked over and prodded one of the tree trunks with her finger.

"They're just tree trunks," she called back to McCools.

"Yes, but *they* are not," said McCools, pointing to an opening in the cliff face.

There stood the two Tree Trolls holding up a paralysed unicorn, another lying on the ground beside them and Blade fluttering frantically inside a glass jar.

"Don't worry, I'm coming," shouted Thumble Tumble, running towards Blade, her wand directed at the Tree Trolls.

"Stop!" hollered McCools, just as her foot entered the concealed lasso. She was catapulted up into the air by her ankle, and then, hanging upside-down ten feet off the ground, she watched her captors reveal themselves.

Ugg stepped away from his tree first, shaking off some excess bark. Ogg then peeled himself off from the tree right beside him, holding a small cage that he shoved over McCools' head.

"Reveal this," Ugg laughed as he walked over to the entrance of the cave and pulled the stone eyes off the trees that they had disguised as themselves.

Thumble Tumble was furious that she hadn't noticed they were walking into a trap. She dangled upside down, listening to the two greedy trolls discussing their fate.

"We'll eat the haggis for tea," grinned Ugg, rubbing his belly.

"What about the girl?" asked Ogg, smacking his lips.

"She's for Mogdred," Ugg relpied. "When we give her Thumble Tumble, she'll reward us for sure!"

Chapter 21

Fairy Tug

Serena awoke with a pounding headache. She had landed head first after being hit by the 'lightning bolt'. The fall had knocked her out, rendering her unconscious for the full day.

"I know exactly what you want from Gracie," she mumbled to herself as she started to come round. "You want her bracelet so that you can see into the future, now that you no longer have your all-seeing globe."

A single tear rolled down her cheek as she murmured these words to herself. She knew that if Mogdred got her hands on Gracie's bracelet, she would never be able to free her sister from the evil clutches of the Night Witch.

When the pounding in her head subsided, she realised she was miles away from the Holy Isle tug boat.

"Oh, no," she gasped, and started galloping as fast as she could through the Light and Dark Forest towards the shore.

It was eerily quiet when she arrived at the empty jetty.

The boat was gone… she would never make it to the Holy Isle on time.

"No!" she screamed up into the night sky.

"Can I help you?" asked a young girl who seemed to have appeared from nowhere. The girl had pale blue eyes, white hair and skin to match.

"Not unless you have a boat," Serena replied sarcastically.

"You mean, like this one?" asked the girl, gesturing to a small tug tied to the jetty.

"As long as you can pay, you can sail," she added.

"What's the price?" Serena probed suspiciously.

"Magic" the girl replied, holding out her hand.

Serena plucked a single strand of violet hair from her head and handed to the girl. "This is Deer Folk hair."

"This will take you one quarter of the way," the girl said, frowning at the single hair stand on her palm.

Serena grasped a clump of hair and pulled. "Ouch!" she yelled as a dozen strands came out at once. She placed the clump of hair on the girl's hand and was instantly granted access to the tug boat, via the gang plank at the rear.

The tug was small, with room for about four passengers plus the captain. On this journey, Serena was the only passenger. The girl pulled up the anchor, then sprinkled some dust in the air. The tug moved off the jetty and started floating across the water towards the Holy Isle.

"There's no need to stay in disguise on my account," Serena said.

"I beg your pardon," the girl retorted.

"I said there's no need…"

"I know what you said," replied the girl, abruptly cutting her off. "Aren't you Mogdred's sidekick?"

"Not everything is what it seems," said Serena. "I though *you* of all people would appreciate that!"

The girl stared at Serena. Her body glowed bright red then burst into thin air, leaving a tiny winged fairy hovering in her place. The little fairy was five centimetres tall and looked almost transparent.

Loxi was a rogue Water Fairy who had run away to see the world. Unfortunately, she had quickly found out that water fairies cannot survive beyond the boundaries of Arran, and so she'd taken up position as captain of the tug (or *Fairy Tug*, as it's better known on the island). This was so that each day, as she crossed over the water to the Holy Isle, she could imagine she was going on an adventure to some faraway, mysterious land.

Loxi suddenly grabbed hold of the wheel and turned the tug sharply to the left. The jolt almost sent Serena flying into the water.

"Apologies for that," Loxi said, "but we definitely don't want to end up in the Lurgie." She indicated the dark patch of murky water they'd just managed to avoid.

The remainder of the journey was fairly calm and Serena stood at the back of the tug, quietly scribbling notes onto a piece of parchment.

When they arrived at the Holy Isle, Loxi once again put on her disguise. She secured the tug to the shore with a rope and lowered the gang plank. Serena rolled up the piece of parchment and tucked it inside her top before trotting off the tug. She turned to thank Loxi. Both the tug, and Loxi had vanished!

"Fairies," Serena smiled to herself, then headed along the shoreline.

She arrived at the Eagalach Stadium two hours later, just in time to see the Thistle Pixies walk onto the pitch for the second half of the game.

Scoutt took up his position in the centre circle, waiting for Dazzler to join him. He was completely taken aback as Slayer led the Cornflower players onto the pitch, the bright blue captain's armband stretched around his biceps.

In Slayer's position as keeper stood an equally massive pixie, also wearing a Skull and Crossbones on his bib. Horace, nicknamed Head Basher, was Slayer's best friend. He liked nothing more than bashing people on the head.

The referee took a head count of the teams. "You only have eight players," he said to Scoutt. "Why don't you bring on your substitutes?"

"They seem to have disappeared," replied Scoutt, scowling towards Slayer. Slayer sniggered back at him.

"And you know the rules, ref," Slayer observed gleefully. "You can't change your substitutes after the first whistle has blown... not even if they've mysteriously vanished," he finished with a menacing laugh.

The referee looked straight into Slayer's eyes, unfazed

by his mammoth size.

"I know you are cheating," he said quietly. "And when I catch you, you'll be off this pitch faster than the Bolt Ball."

"Are you threatening me, ref?" snorted Slayer.

"Oh, no. I'm deadly serious," replied the referee. He then blew his golden whistle right in Slayer's face as he released the ball.

This time the ball was facing the Cornflower goal and it ran towards the net like an Olympian. The Cornflower runners might as well have been taking a leisurely stroll, as they failed miserably to get anywhere near it.

Slayer was dashing after the ball, which was just making it run even faster.

Head Basher was in position with his legs spread and arms out.

"Stop chasing the ball!" Mr Frankenhouzen was screaming from the side-lines.

Slayer turned to hear what his manager was shouting. The referee also glanced over to see what Mr Frankenhouzen was screaming about, and as he did, one of the Cornflower Clinchers ran onto the pitch, grabbed the ball and spun it around one hundred and eighty degrees, before running back to the side-lines.

The Bolt Ball ran straight through Slayer's legs, now aiming for the Thistle Pixie goal. Blurr was on its tail. The ball was only a few feet from the goal when Blurr caught up with it. He stretched his leg back to kick it away, and was thrown straight off the pitch by Slayer, who grabbed him by the ankle and swung him right over his head.

Rocky was so distracted by Slayer's blatant foul he didn't notice the Bolt Ball running between his feet.

'GOAL' the stadium speakers rung out. This was followed by a short burst of the Cornflower anthem, then the huge screen at the far end of the stadium lit up:

Thistle Pixies – 0
Cornflower Pixies – 1

The referee rounded on Slayer.

"That's it, your off!" he shouted, directing Slayer to the side-lines.

"What?" Slayer stood holding his hands above his head, as if in disbelief.

"He tripped over his shoelaces. *Didn't he, Klein?* he snarled at the tiny clincher standing beside Blurr's mangled body.

"Don't bother answering that," snapped the referee, "unless you want to be sent off too… for corroborating a cheat. I saw the whole thing myself this time." "Then you saw wrong" Slayer blared into his face.

The referee pulled his shoulders back, pushing out his chest, and rose to his full height. He still looked tiny standing in Slayers daunting shadow.

"Bullies don't frighten me… and you're nothing but a big bully. Now get off this pitch before I extend your ten-match ban into a ban for life."

"You can't do that," protested Slayer.

"Watch me," said the referee, still pointing towards the side-lines.

Slayer marched off the pitch, kicking up clumps of grass and shouting back empty threats of having the referee fired.

The referee completely ignored Slayer, who was acting

like a petulant child, and walked over to Blurr.

"Do you think you can play?" he enquired.

Blurr nodded his head... then passed out. The Thistle Pixies were down to seven players, against the ten-strong Cornflower Pixie team.

Klein stepped in as captain of the Cornflower team and shook Scoutt's hand, indicating there would be no more cheating under his watch.

The referee blew the whistle, and once again the Bolt Ball tore off down the pitch aiming for the Thistle Pixie goal. There were only three Thistle Pixies actually on the pitch, Scoutt, Snoddy and Sprint, the other remaining runner.

The four Thistle Pixie clinchers looked on helplessly from the side-lines as they watched their team mates race up the pitch after the ball. Scoutt swooped in from just in front of the net and sent the ball hurtling in the opposite direction.

All of the Thistle Pixie runners were now in their own half of the pitch, and so the ball decided to have a quick two-minute rest. It leaned over to catch its breath and as it did, Head Basher came hurtling towards it from behind. The Bolt Ball zoomed through the air like a rocket and landed just centimetres in front of the Thistle Pixie goal. It stood up – then fell into the net.

'GOAL' the speakers echoed through the stadium. But instead of the usual blast of the scoring team's anthem, there was a loud roar of thunder. The night sky turned pitch black and the lights around the stadium started to go out one at a time, until they were in complete darkness.

Thistle Pixies – 0
Cornflower Pixies – 2

The score flashed up on the screen at the far end of the pitch, illuminating the stadium for a split second before it exploded as a Thunderbolt hit it dead centre.

The spectators were screaming as they tried to make their way to the exits in the dark. The sky flared periodically, as ream after ream of Thunderbolts came cascading down on the stadium.

With each blast, the pixies caught a glimpse of their attackers. The sky was littered with Night Witches and Troll Witches firing down on them.

"We need to light the exits," Kyle, the chief of the Thistle Pixies, hollered to his clansmen.

The chief had been watching the game and was now running with a handful of glow-worms towards the exits. Armed with flashing glow-worms, his clansmen were also working their way through the screaming crowds towards the exits.

"How did they get past the unicorn barrier?" one of the clansmen asked Kyle.

"I don't know. But as soon as we get these exits illuminated I want you to prepare the men for battle. I'll go to the caves and see what's happened."

The last Night Witch to arrive on the scene was Mogdred, flanked by her two loathsome daughters, Sloth and Gretch.

"Don't fire onto the pitch," she ordered. "I need the female player alive."

She shot a spark into the sky, lighting it up with a red glow. This was the sign for Serena to take Gracie.

Mogdred watched intently from the skies above as Serena made her way onto the pitch.

All of the players were standing in a circle around

Gracie. They had heard Mogdred's order to capture her.

"Give me the girl," Serena said, looking at the impenetrable wall of Thistle Pixies and Cornflower Pixies.

"You'll have to get through us first," Snoddy said fiercely.

"Mogdred will kill you all. Please just hand over the girl."

"Never," Scoutt replied boldly.

Then out of the corner of his eye he saw Head Basher grab Gracie by the wrist and thrust her out of the circle towards Serena.

"I'm not dying for some Thistle Pixie," Head Basher said.

"You fool!" shouted Scoutt. "You've just signed all of our death warrants."

From the skies above, they heard Mogdred's final order. "Kill them... k*ill them all!*" she shrieked. And with that, a hail of Death Bolts flooded the sky.

Chapter 22

Haggis for Tea

Ugg and Ogg placed a large pile of driftwood under McCools' cage and set it alight. They then sat on the ground beside the fire as their dinner slowly roasted.

"I want a leg," Ogg said, dribbling saliva onto the ground.

"Well he has three, so I don't see that being a problem," Ugg laughed as he sprinkled some herbs over the cage.

"Let him go!" screamed Thumble Tumble, still dangling upside down. As she writhed and wriggled, the wand fell out of her cloak and into her hand.

"It's all your fault," she squealed at the wand. She was ready to throw it away when she said, "You'll just come straight back again, won't you? You'll do the *exact* opposite of what I want!"

She stopped ranting for a moment. "That's it," she thought to herself.

She aimed the wand at the fire underneath McCools and shouted "Extingusto!" A red-hot flame shot out of the end of the wand and hit the fire. Instead of being extinguished, the fire grew into a mini inferno, sending sparks all over the place.

"Thanks for that," sniggered Ogg. "Our dinner will be ready in half the time now." Just then, one of the sparks hit him slap bang on the bottom and set him on fire. "*Arrrgh!*" he screamed, as he ran past Ugg towards the waters' edge.

Ugg burst out laughing at the sight of Ogg's flaming bottom, and as he did a spark landed right inside his open mouth, setting fire to his tongue. He ran after his twin brother, crying out in agony.

The flames under McCools were getting higher and had begun to singe his orange fur.

Another huge spark shot out of the fire, and this time it landed on the rope holding Thumble Tumble. The flame snaked down towards her foot, hissing as it slithered. Its forked tongue licked her heel just as the fire burned through the rope, sending Thumble Tumble head-first to the ground.

As soon as she landed she raced over to the fire and started kicking dirt on it to put out the flames. But they were too strong, and continued barbecuing her friend.

She scanned the ground frantically, looking for anything to help put out the fire. But the only thing she could see was her red cloak, which had fallen off when she crashed to the ground.

"Cold when it's hot!" she shouted, and she grabbed the cloak and threw it onto the fire. Within seconds, the flames disappeared under the cloak. Thumble Tumble pulled the cage off McCools. "Are you alright?" she gasped anxiously.

"A little singed but otherwise I'm fine," he replied

smiling. "Thank goodness for your Auntie Isla's all-weather cloak."

"It does exactly what it says on the label," Thumble Tumble laughed back.

The two friends then ran over to the cave entrance, and released Blade from the glass jar.

"What happened to the unicorns?" asked Thumble Tumble.

"It was Mogdred," Blade replied. "She used the Sleeping Death Curse on them."

McCools' head dropped as soon as Blade mentioned the Sleeping Death Curse. He knew Thumble Tumble would not have come across such an evil curse before.

"What do we do?" she asked McCools.

"I don't think there's much we can do," he replied sadly. "Not without the counter curse."

Blade fluttered back into the jar and re-emerged almost instantly. "Maybe this can help," he announced, holding out a piece of rolled up parchment. "Someone sneaked this into the jar whilst I was sleeping," he explained.

"What makes you think it can help us?" asked McCools.

"Because it says, 'Sleeping Death Counter Curse' along the outside," Blade said, pointing to the outside of the scroll.

McCools took the scroll, which had been tied by a single strand of violet hair. He carefully untied it and unrolled the parchment to reveal the words of the counter curse.

"Here," he said to Thumble Tumble, handing it to her. "Only a great witch can perform the counter curse."

"But I'm not a great witch," replied Thumble Tumble hesitantly.

"You are the Protector," McCools said, clasping her hands in his. "Now, protect us!" Thumble Tumble read out the counter curse:

"Evil's will shall be undone,
From the sky, I command the power of the sun."

Her body started to tremble and the earth below her feet started to shake. She took a deep breath and continued reading the words written on the piece of parchment.

"Darkened forces have done their worst,
But with the light, I reverse this curse."

A green light rose-up from the ground beneath her feet and surrounded her as she started to float up into the air. Beams of light shot out of her body covering the unicorns in an emerald halo. As the light passed over the unicorns, they began to wake from their deathly slumber.

They slowly opened their eyes, then shakily stood up on all four legs.

When the final beam of light passed through Thumble Tumble, her eyes glazed over and her body went limp, before falling to the ground.

She had awoken the unicorns, and as they returned to life, so too did their Magical Barrier.

The hail of Death Bolts hurtling towards the Eagalach pitch suddenly rebounded off an invisible forcefield, vaporising the attacking Night Witches.

One by one the Night Witches were transformed into piles of ash as their own bolts boomeranged back towards them. Empty brooms crashed onto the pitch below.

"Run!" Scoutt shouted.

The players sprinted off the pitch towards the changing rooms, zigzagging to avoid the falling brooms that were raining down on them like javelin poles.

Snoddy and Scoutt grabbed hold of Serena. "You're coming with us," Scoutt said as he tried to tie her hands together using his armband.

Serena kicked up with her front legs, but just then a broom came crashing down on her back, knocking her out cold.

Tabathay looked down in disbelief as she watched her ground-troops completely disintegrate. The Magical Barrier had engulfed every witch below it, reducing them to piles of dust as it swept its way back across the Holy Isle.

"The barrier has been restored," Tabathay screamed. From where she was flying above the magical forcefield, she desperately looked around the skies for Mogdred to receive her orders. But Mogdred was gone.

She was already flying out to sea with her two daughters, surrounded by a violent storm created by her own rage.

Chapter 23

The Interrogation

"She's breathing," Blade cried out to McCools as he fluttered just above Thumble Tumble's mouth.

Thumble Tumble was lying lifeless on the ground, still clenching the piece of parchment in her hand.

"Get back," shouted Kyle, pointing at Blade with his spear as he emerged from the thick grass. Kyle had arrived just in time to see Thumble Tumble free the unicorns from Mogdred's evil curse.

"No way," replied Blade, putting up his fists to defend his helpless friend.

"It's OK," said McCools, taking hold of Blade's foot and lowering him to the ground. "He's here to help."

"How, by screeching her back to life?" snapped Blade.

"She's not dead," said McCools. "She's just sleeping. But she's in a sleep so deep that she cannot wake from it by herself. You see, when she performed the counter curse, the Sleeping Death transferred to her."

"Why on earth did you let her do it then?" Blade yelled.

"Because she was the only one who *could* do it," McCools retorted. "Do you think I like to see her like this? Now *please,* stand back and let the chief through."

Kyle slowly walked past Thumble Tumble's body towards the unicorns. He stopped a few feet in front of them and bowed so low that his hair touched the ground.

The unicorns both responded by tapping their hooves three times. Kyle removed the piece of parchment from Thumble Tumble's grasp and showed it to the unicorns. In response, they backed away from him, shaking their manes.

"Is that it?" Blade screamed angrily. "I thought he was here to help us!"

Kyle shot him a piercing glance. "Shh," he said, nodding towards the cave entrance.

Standing in the entrance was a third unicorn. He was much smaller than the other two, only a foal. The two older unicorns walked their foal over to Thumble Tumble's body, then took a step back.

The young foal gazed down at her for a few seconds, opened his mouth and blew a stream of icy breath straight onto Thumble Tumble's white lips.

As the unicorn's breath touched her lips, they began to twitch. She pursed her lips, then opened her mouth wide and inhaled a massive gasp of air. After a few more seconds, her eyelids began fluttering, and finally opened. As she sat up, the foal retreated to join his parents.

"Thank you," said McCools, bending over. This was as close to a bow as he could manage with his round body.

All three unicorns returned the gesture, before heading home to their Emerald Woodland, deep within the cave.

As soon as they had gone, Kyle helped Thumble

Tumble to her feet.

"We need to get back to the Eagalach Stadium," he said, in a tone of urgency.

"It's this way," he directed, and they all sped through the long grass towards the village.

"I thought only a 'Great Witch' had the power to reverse the Sleeping Death Curse," Blade quizzed McCools, as they raced through the grass.

"That's right," gasped McCools, trying to keep pace.

"Then how did the unicorn manage it?"

"Only a great witch can reverse the Sleeping Death Curse. But, the magical kiss of a unicorn foal can bring any child back to life," McCools panted, on the point of collapse from all the exertion.

"Oh, I see," said Blade, feeling enlightened.

Smoke was still bellowing from the stadium where the thunderbolts had struck, but at least the emergency glow-worm lighting was now up and running.

"What's the damage?" asked Kyle, as he ran through the entrance.

"Thirty-one casualties, no fatalities, chief," replied one of his clansmen.

"Thank goodness," gasped Kyle.

"And Gracie, is she OK?"

"Yes chief. She's with her team mates in the changing room. We've thrown that coward, Head Basher, in jail, and have the female Deer Folk tied up on the pitch ready for questioning.

Kyle marched onto the pitch with McCools, Blade and Thumble Tumble in tow.

He pulled out his spear and held it under Serena's chin, tipping her head up so that he could look into her eyes as he interrogated her.

"Who are you?"

Serena didn't answer.

He pressed his spear further into her chin.

"I asked you a question," Kyle roared.

She just continued to stare blankly, without uttering a word.

Kyle grabbed her by the shoulders and started shaking her. "Who… are… you?" he bellowed.

As her head tipped back, tresses of her long violet hair fell over her face.

"Her name is Serena," McCools said. "She is one of Mogdred's henchmen, as far as I know." He began pacing up and down in front of Serena. "The thing I don't know, is why she helped us. It was you who left the counter curse for us."

"I did not," Serena protested.

"Yes, you did," McCools replied adamantly. "I'd recognise this hair anywhere." He produced the strand of purple hair that the roll of parchment had been tied with.

"Please… Mogdred cannot find out I helped you," Serena pleaded. "If she finds out, she'll kill my sister!" Tears streamed down her face as she told them how Mogdred had snatched Alfy and was now holding her prisoner in her dungeon.

"If I don't do Mogdred's bidding, she'll take Alfy's life," she continued, sobbing.

"Is there no way to free her?" asked Kyle.

"I've tried," explained Serena. "But Mogdred's lair is hidden under a veil of dark magic. The only way in or out is with one of Mogdred's lightning bolts.

"Maybe not," intervened McCools. "But we'd need to

act quickly," he looked over at Kyle anxiously, "before Mogdred returns to her lair."

Kyle untied Serena. "Go," he said. "I have a sister too, and there is nothing I wouldn't do for her!"

"Can you gallop?" asked McCools.

"Yes" Serena replied.

Thumble Tumble and McCools climbed onto her back, and the three of them sped off in the direction of the beach. Meanwhile, Blade helped the Thistle Pixies clear the pitch, ready to resume play of the Eagalach Cup Final.

McCools guided Serena back to the site of the conjuring and they disembarked beside the three symbols.

He picked up a twig. "What do we etch onto the points of the pentagon?" he asked Serena.

"Stars," she replied. "Five stars, to represent the five levels of the Underworld."

McCools quickly etched the outlines of five new stars into the sand, one at each tip of the pentagon.

"Can you remember the spell?" he asked, rummaging around in his scarf looking for something.

"Yes, but you need a heart for the conjuring," said Serena, "and we have no time to find one," she continued, pulling the small dagger out from her waist.

"You'll have to use mine," she said, and thrust the dagger into the air with the blade pointing towards her chest.

Thumble Tumble jumped up and grabbed hold of her hand.

"Stop!" she yelled.

"Let me go," Serena demanded as she struggled to break free from Thumble Tumble's remarkably strong grip.

McCools was still feeling around in his scarf as Thumble Tumble wrestled with Serena. Then he shouted out triumphantly "Got it!" and held out a small heart in the palm of his hand.

Serena's jaw fell open in amazement. She stopped struggling. "How?" she gasped.

"Didn't you know all Haggis have two hearts?" replied Thumble Tumble chirpily. "One for using, and one for emergencies… and I'd say this is an emergency!"

McCools placed his spare heart into the centre symbol.

"What if it doesn't work?" asked Serena looking nervous.

"It'll work," he whispered, as he dropped some dirt into her hand.

Serena stepped forward and intoned:

"*Oh Lord of the Darkness hear my call,*
My sister I conjure, most loving of all,
To you the moon and the stars I bring,
Along with this heart, as an offering."

She threw the dirt into the circle and all three of them watched in wonder as Alfy's body slowly rose from the ground beneath the symbol.

"Alfy, you're alive!" Serena cried, and she threw her arms around her sister.

Alfy emerged from the circle completely unscathed. Well, apart from her hair. Instead of having flowing purple locks, she was now sporting a spiky orange mop!

Chapter 24

The Cup Final

Thumble Tumble and McCools left Serena and Alfy at the *Fairy Tug* before returning to the Eagalach stadium. They arrived just as the last of the stands were being put back into place for the remaining three minutes of the Eagalach Cup Final.

"I was wondering why I haven't disintegrated," Thumble Tumble said to McCools, as they were shown to their VIP seating beside Kyle, the chief of the Thistle Pixies.

"You are immune to the Magical Barrier now," said McCools. "Once you've been kissed by a unicorn, you are no longer affected by their magic."

"Phew, just as well you knew that," she sighed.

"I'd actually forgotten that you would frazzle when the unicorns awoke, to be honest. It's just as well the Sleeping Death Curse passed on to you, or you probably would have!" McCools smiled cheekily, and then took his seat for the game.

The Thistle Pixies were back up to nine players

with the release of their two kidnapped substitutes. The Cornflower Pixies were also playing with a team of nine, after the removal of Slayer and Head Basher from the team.

There was an eerie quiet in the stadium as the two captains shook hands.

"This is so exciting!" exclaimed Thumble Tumble, from her bird's-eye view of the pitch.

The referee blew his golden whistle and the Bolt Ball was off and running. It left its box so quickly, Thumble Tumble didn't actually see it run out.

From the loudspeaker above her head, she could hear the commentator giving a blow-by-blow account of the action on the pitch.

"With just three minutes remaining, the atmosphere here in the Holy Isle Stadium is electric. Snoddy is chasing the ball... now Fredrick... now Blurr... and it's out! The Bolt Ball has been caught by Klein. Great catch by the tiny clincher."

The commentary was non-stop as the bolt ball whizzed back and forth between the two goals.

"What's the score?" asked Thumble Tumble.

"Two-nil to the Cornflower Pixies," replied Kyle, pointing to the replacement big screen that had been erected at the far side of the stadium.

"The clock is ticking down as we enter the last minute of play..." the commentator proclaimed, "and the ball is heading straight for the Thistle Pixie goal. It's on target. *Great save by Rocky the Thistle Pixie keeper*," the commentator shouted as Rocky headed the ball off the pitch.

Thumble Tumble and McCools were transfixed by the action on and off the pitch as they watched Gracie zoom along the side-lines.

"The ball is out… and it's between Gracie and Klein," the commentary continued.

"Which of these agile clinchers will catch it? It's looking like Klein has the edge. Wait a minute. The ball has just changed direction, unbelievably it seems to be running straight into Gracie's hands."

Gracie caught the ball with just fifteen seconds remaining on the clock. She took a deep breath and then threw it with all her might towards the Cornflower goal. Snoddy and Blurr both raced after the ball.

"Oh no, Blurr has taken a tumble," said the commentator as Blurr plunged face first into the grass.

The Bolt Ball was just two feet away from the Cornflower goal.

"If Snoddy doesn't get a touch of the ball, even if we score, we lose!" said Kyle, his hands in front of his eyes, watching the game through the spaces between his fingers.

"How come?" asked Thumble Tumble, without taking her eyes off the game.

"If the ball runs into the goal on its own, we get one point. But, if we kick it in, we get three points, and we need three points to win," Kyle explained, still watching the game through his fingers.

"It looks like it's all over for the Thistle Pixies," remarked the commentator. Then, "Hold on!" he roared. "Snoddy's gaining on the ball. Could we be about to witness history?"

"GOAL" rung out across the stadium.

Then over the speakers, the entire stadium could hear the commentator asking his colleagues for clarity.

"What just happened? Did he get a touch?"

The next second, the entire stadium erupted in loud cheering as the large screen flashed up:

Thistle Pixies – 3
Cornflower Pixies – 2

An extended blast of the Thistle Pixie anthem started blaring out.

"He obviously did!" said Kyle, jumping out of his seat. He grabbed McCools around the waist and lifted him up off the ground, then started dancing with him, before turning and doing the same to Thumble Tumble.

The cheering, dancing and random hugging among the Thistle Pixie fans continued for twenty minutes solid. Kyle then headed onto the pitch to present the trophies.

Each of the runners-up received a silver medal, mined from the ancient dwarf mountains. The players of the winning team, along with their manager, were each presented with a medal cast from goblin's gold, as well as the magnificent Eagalach Cup.

The Eagalach Cup was carved from a single ruby, and it sent rays of crimson spiralling through the stadium, reflecting the light from the glow-worm illuminations.

First up were the Cornflower Pixies. The players walked onto the pitch with their heads down, but the spectators all rose to their feet and cheered them for their valiant efforts.

With their spirits raised, each of the players (although with the noticeable absence of their manager) graciously accepted their runners-up medals from Kyle.

The Thistle Pixie team stepped onto the pitch next, their four injured players being stretchered on. As soon as Snoddy appeared, the cheering, dancing and random hugging recommenced with even more vivacity.

The players who could stand lined up in front of Kyle, while the four injured players sat on their stretchers on the ground, each one with a pixie medic in attendance.

Kyle walked along the line placing a medal over each players head and shaking their hand, with the supporters clapping and cheering every time.

Scoutt accepted the Eagalach Cup on behalf of the Thistle Pixie team. He held the cup high above his head, and this time the cheering was off the scale and the supporters broke into a full-blown Thistle Pixie screech.

"Cover your ears," McCools shouted to Thumble Tumble.

Thankfully, Kyle had already anticipated that there might be the risk of a Thistle Pixie screech, and had provided Thumble Tumble with a set of magical ear-plugs to ensure her head didn't explode!

Mr Frankenhouzen was below in the Cornflower changing room listening to the wretched noise coming from above. He smashed his hands off the wooden bench in the centre of the room, and they momentarily changed back into the hands of a woman.

"Patience," Miss Malovent said to herself, and quickly morphed back.

In the form of Mr Frankenhouzen, she headed up into the stadium to carry out Mogdred's order:

"Find Thumble Tumble. And *kill her!*"

www.thumbletumble.co.uk
Find out more about this series, latest news, events and
when the next book will be available.

All books in the series can be ordered from the Thumble
Tumble website and are also available from your local
bookshop and online retailers.
www.scottishbookstore.com

Or by post from:
Thumble Tumble, PO Box 27132 Glasgow G3 9ER
Email:info@thumbletumble.co.uk

Follow the Adventure!

Don't miss books one and two of the Thumble Tumble series, *Thumble Tumble and the Ollpheist* and *Thumble Tumble and the Cauldron of Undry*.

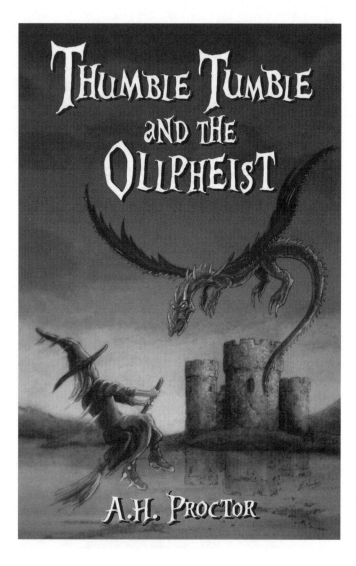

THUMBLE TUMBLE
and the
OLIPHEIST

A.H. PROCTOR

THUMBLE TUMBLE
AND THE
CAULDRON OF UNDRY

A.H. PROCTOR

About the Author

A.H. Proctor is a successful businesswoman, wife and mother who has unashamedly lived in a fantasy world for most of her life. Captivated from childhood by fairy stories and the world of the Brothers Grimm, her fertile imagination was held in check until she took her own young children to the beautiful and mystical Isle of Arran. When, one day, they asked her to tell them a story of witches and dragons, the floodgates opened. Inevitably, Angela could not resist taking it a stage further and she began to write, and so the Thumble Tumble books set on mysterious Arran were born.